Unreal City

Neil Powell's publications include three collections of poems - *At the Edge* (1977), *A Season of Calm Weather* (1982) and *True Colours* (1991) - and a critical study of contemporary British poetry, *Carpenters of Light* (1979). He edited the *Selected Poems* of Fulke Greville (1990). He has contributed poetry, fiction, essays and reviews to numerous magazines and newspapers, and has broadcast on BBC Radio 3 and local radio stations; in 1988 he was an Eastern Arts Writer in Residence and in 1989 a tutor at the Arvon Foundation. He has been a teacher and a bookseller, and is now a freelance writer working on a second novel and on a critical biography of Roy Fuller.

By the same author

Poetry
At the Edge
A Season of Calm Weather
True Colours

Criticism
Carpenters of Light

Selected Poems of Fulke Greville
(Edited with an introduction by Neil Powell)

Unreal City

Neil Powell

Millivres Books
Brighton

First published in 1992 by Millivres Books (Publishers),
33 Bristol Gardens, Brighton BN2 5JR, East Sussex, England

Copyright © Neil Powell 1992
The moral right of the author has been asserted

ISBN 1 873741 04 9

Typeset by Hailsham Typesetting Services,
Wentworth House, George Street, Hailsham, E. Sussex

Printed by Billing & Sons Ltd, Worcester

Distributed in the United Kingdom and Western Europe by
Turnaround Distribution Co-Op Ltd, 27 Horsell Road,
London N5 1XL

for Ian Sizeland

Author's Note

Malcolm Bradbury once prefaced a novel with the unbeatable disclaimer, 'This is a book, and what it says is not true.' This is a book, too, and most of what it says is not true. All the characters in it, including holders of public office, are imaginary; no-one who feels I have borrowed gestures or details from them should rashly assume that I have stolen the rest of them. There is no new Public Order Act (yet) and no secret police department called RAID (I hope). There is no Salisbury Road in N 17 nor, as far as I know, a pub called The Clarendon near wherever Salisbury Road might have been. But Covent Garden, Earl's Court and Aldeburgh do exist, and where I have used real locations for my fictional narrative I have tried to do so with reasonable accuracy.

'I'm Not Scared' by Chris Lowe and Neil Tennant© 1988 Cage Music Ltd/10 Music Ltd.
'Sometimes' by Vince Clarke and Andy Bell© 1986 Sonet Publishing Ltd.

What, in fact, is a novel but a universe in which action is endowed with form, where final words are pronounced, where people possess one another completely and where life assumes the aspect of destiny? The world of the novel is only a rectification of the world we live in, in pursuance of man's deepest wishes. For the world is undoubtedly the same one we know. The suffering, the illusion, the love are the same. The heroes speak our language, have our weaknesses and our strength. Their universe is neither more beautiful nor more enlightening than ours.

Albert Camus: *The Rebel*

Man is in love and loves what vanishes,
What more is there to say?

W.B.Yeats: *Nineteen Hundred and Nineteen*

ONE

As the light flickered and dimmed once again, Clive reached across and hit the side of the Anglepoise shade. This time the lamp went out entirely, the bulb rattled and fell hotly onto his desk. He gingerly pushed it aside, at the same time feeling sorry, with his sentimental regard for certain objects, for the bulbless lamp which now reared its stupid long neck towards the ceiling. The Anglepoise was old and quite possibly valuable - it had been second-hand when, as a student, he had bought it - but he cherished it simply as an anachronistic survivor, an obstinate relic like himself. It was in a sense fortunate that his office or studio or spare room, at any rate the place in which he fitfully worked, was also lit by a fluorescent tube, for while he had been immersed in a pool of variable light dusk had gathered rapidly and it was now almost dark outside.

It was raining too. Clive heard the insistent trickle and splash from the rusted gutter down the wrong side of a drainpipe and onto the lid of a dustbin at the back of the house. One day when it wasn't raining he ought at least to move the dustbin: one day. A police siren, or just possibly an ambulance, wailed along the dead-end street at the front of the house. He automatically moved towards the window to look out, but he was too late and in any case too high up, on the second floor, to see into the street without actually pressing his face against the glass. From his desk, in this deepening twilight, it was almost possible to believe that the world outside the window was as it had always been: the upper storeys of the house opposite looked ordinary enough, if a bit shabby; some curtained windows faintly glowed; the streetlamps, mysteriously immune from the fluctuations of the domestic electricity supply, were imperturbably warming from red to amber. Only daylight would reveal the shabbiness as advanced decay.

Only a different perspective would disclose the boarded-up shopfronts and rubbish-heaped pavements.

That siren had troubled him: the interminable repetition of the noise might have led to unconcern in other citizens, but in Clive it induced the increasingly obsessive conviction that, sooner or later, the next one would be for him. You heard intermittent and excited rumours that they were about to start picking people up, and one day it would surely happen. That afternoon, outside the tube, there had been a couple of plain-clothes men, looking for someone like him. He had been into Soho for a lunchtime drink with a publisher. Returning, hot and headachy, he trudged up the unmoving escalator and there they were, on the other side of the automatic barrier, with their rugby builds and too-perfect composure. He felt their disinterested looks follow him across and down the street, didn't want to turn to see the picture snapped, the note jotted or spoken into a radio.

He reached home safely enough, of course. In Salisbury Road there was nothing more threatening than a bony Burmese cat and a dishevelled woman poking into a rubbish bag that smelled of very old curry, but paranoia was where you lived these days. Once inside the flat, he made coffee and thought about making phone calls, leafing through a much-updated address book which was like an alphabeticised autobiography. He tried calling Jeremy in Suffolk, to whom a mutation of his own unfocussed panic ought to have spread since the Sizewell accident, but got no reply. Colin in Putney, whose number he tried next, was engaged and would typically remain that way for at least an hour. He put on an old vinyl record of Lucia Popp singing the *Four Last Songs*, its scratches and clicks as familiarly reassuring as the dog and trumpet on the label. Work had to be done. In a corner beside his desk was a tall stack of books - the bottom ones might well be out of print by now - which he was supposed to review. A bursting buff folder contained the typescript of a book entitled *The Radical Urge: Literature and Liberation in the Late Twentieth Century* which he was supposed to be copy-editing for the

2

impoverished publisher. And strewn about him was the half-finished artwork for the next issue of *Pendulum*, the quarterly which he jointly, often solely, edited and which the nameless bosses of the plain-clothes policemen would have liked to see quickly extinguished. As usual, *Pendulum* won his loyalty against his better financial judgement. Quite apart from the content, the process pleased him: the typesetting on an obsolete IBM Selectric composer thrown out, and donated, by a sympathetic local printer; the tricks still to be played with Letraset; the stripping-in of photographs. The simplicity and physicality of the tools - Rotring pen, Stanley knife, steel ruler - appealed to him in a time of abstract electronic technology. They had the honest incorruptability of the Anglepoise lamp.

After an hour's absorbed labour, Clive remembered that he needed to shop: for himself tonight, and for Kieran too over the weekend. Since the corner shop had closed down, this meant driving or walking to the superstore which, with its acres of car park, occupied a former light industrial site half a mile or so away. Despite the prospect of an encumbered return journey, he walked it. From the outside, the store was a whimsical nostalgic fantasy, all odd gables and redundant beams; inside, it was like any other supermarket, rectangular and efficient. Entering it, Clive always felt cheated, the victim of a malevolent alchemy: the architects promised human individuality but delivered merely a disinfected version of the production lines which had once rightfully belonged here. The shoppers, mostly middle-aged women pushing trolleys which overflowed with bright packages, seemed to accept this world with a resignation which made Clive envious and furious. As he browsed, self-contained, a girl dressed mostly in tinfoil diamonds accosted him: 'Excuse me, sir,' she said, speaking like a deranged answerphone, 'but have you tried new Silver Diamond Low Fat Spread?' 'No,' he snapped, 'and I come here for food, not propaganda.' He strode on, angry with himself for rising to the bait. 'I thought you were a vegetarian,' said a more familiar voice. It was Karen, from Babel Translators, peering into his basket and discovering beef ill-concealed beneath the peppers, aubergines and onions. 'Hello, yes you know I am,' he said. 'I suppose you're cooking for some carnivorous boy again,' she grinned. 'Lucky you.' And she vanished into the crowd, a momentary glimpse of mildly refreshing anarchy. Minutes later, they passed again: she was reading the small print on the yoghurt pots. 'You'd like him. He's called Kieran - it's almost an anagram. You must come round for a meal sometime,' he said. 'Help me make an honest vegetarian of him.'

He headed for the checkouts. He chose not quite the shortest queue: there was a boy called Philip, still in the sixth-form at school, who worked here some afternoons. Clive saw him sometimes in the pub or on the street - tight jeans, battered leather jacket, very neat long blond hair - and was always strangely charmed by his transmogrification into a supermarket cashier. As Philip ran the items over the scanner, Clive adopted his usual attitude of ironic amazement at this miracle of technology, even though he was mostly amazed by Philip's ability to look stunning even when stuck behind a till in a Tesco uniform. 'Incredible,' said Clive, as the itemised printout was passed to him. 'See you later,' said Philip, meaning absolutely nothing.

Outside the store, sheltering under the canopy from a light drizzle, were two more plain-clothes men: they might easily have been the same two, although this time one had a distinctly newly-fledged look about him. There was something almost winsome about that, as if the innocent fluff of an untainted youth had been only recently and incompletely eradicated. Yet they, so Clive heard from friends who had suffered closer encounters with them than he, were the worst to deal with, the keenest to demonstrate their allegiance to the brave if elusive new cause of state security. He walked on briskly, switching the heavy bag of shopping from arm to arm and wondering idly why his left arm tired of the weight so very much more rapidly than his right. When he reached Salisbury Road, the bony Burmese was investigating the curry-flavoured rubbish and the drizzle was becoming more purposeful. He cooked pasta and a wickedly spicy sauce of his own devising, then settled back to some work before drinking time. He tried not to contemplate what the fuck Kieran was up to tonight.

After a while, the phone emitted its apology for a ring.

'Hello, Clive Greenslade.'

'Hi Clive, it's Jeremy. How's things?'

'The same. Damp, dismal, depressed. In other words, sober and overworked. How about you?'

'Oh fine. I still can't quite believe it, but fine.'

Jeremy Barnes was a poet and part-time teacher who lived on the Suffolk coast. When the Sizewell explosion happened, he had been walking his dog along the beach four or five miles away. He had seen the fire, triggered by an electrical fault in an outbuilding, and the miracle was that the radioactive contamination, at least according to the official report, had been negligible. The town in which he lived had been declared completely safe, but it was no longer exactly fashionable: house prices had crashed to the levels of fifteen years earlier, leaving people like him, whose only valuable asset was now vastly devalued, virtually immobilised. Luckily Jeremy, who these days seemed to live inside a huge fisherman's sweater and to share his life with a matching shaggy cream-coloured retriever, had no wish to return to London.

'And Ben?' Clive asked.

'He's great. Keeps me healthy, keeps despair at bay. We've been out along the river to Snape and back. Got wet feet of course. I wish that when God made that river tidal he'd made the tides work in some way I could understand. Ben's still gently steaming.'

'Sounds idyllic. Very Ted Hughes. Okay, very George Crabbe, I know. I tried to call you earlier, but you were obviously busy paddling.'

'Thinking, Clive, thinking, not paddling.'

'Right. Not paddling but thinking. Anyway, I've just pasted up your review for *Pendulum*, and I was wondering if you'd like to do a piece for the next issue.'

'Another review?' Jeremy sounded suspicious.

5

'No, an article. Something subjective, perhaps even autobiographical. Have you ever read Richard Jefferies?'

'Sort of. "Yes, but I ought to re-read him," as my tutor at university used to say when cornered.'

'Good. So you'll know of a book called *After London: Wild England?*'

'Yes, it's the only thing of his I actually possess.'

'That's excellent. What I'm thinking of is an "After London" issue of *Pendulum* which would take a look at that whole idea a century or so later. A sort of symposium by people who've rejected the decaying metropolitan culture and made post-London lives elsewhere. Also I'd like to dent the image of the magazine as the exclusive property of urban homosexuals.'

Jeremy laughed. 'Which of course it is. But I get the drift. Gay life or otherwise among the fish-heads. Or cod-pieces. Let me give it some proper thought. I promise not to produce anything too flippant. Any other stipulations?'

'Length negotiable, peanuts for payment. You know how generous we are.'

'Yes indeed. Anyway, when are you going to forsake this mad metropolis of yours and come and visit me?'

'Soon, soon - towards the end of next week, if you're very unlucky. It's certainly mad. We've got police everywhere, striking dustmen, and power cuts whenever too many people turn their cookers on. But it's all safe and peaceful there?'

'Seems to be. At least they've got back to worrying about oil and sewage again. There was a piece on the local radio this morning about, believe it or not, a raft race at Southend being threatened by pollution. They interviewed a man called Cyril who was organising it. He said: "The sewage at Southend is no worse than it's been for the last thirty years, at least I haven't seen any solid evidence of it." He didn't think he was being funny.'

'Good for Southend Cyril. A total lack of irony is a wonderful strategy for survival.'

'Perhaps. Come and see the wild North Sea soon.'

'I shall. After London.'

Clive returned to his work with diminished energy and enthusiasm. It was an evening on which the uncomplicated elemental forces of air and sea seemed unusually attractive. A dying fly spun uselessly on the desk before him. Then the light flickered and dimmed, and Clive thumped the Anglepoise.

✳ ✳ ✳

In a room of the police lodging-house in Shepherd's Bush, Andrew Symes lay naked on his bed, idly masturbating. Next to him, on a pinboard attached to the wall, was a riot of improbable flesh ripped from magazines, some of which he had seized as pornographic in the course of a recent assignment, together with the day's Page 3 girl from the *Sun*, transfixed by a dart through her left nipple, and a carefully framed photograph of his girlfriend Debbie. She looked serious and mildly disapproving: Andy couldn't be sure whether going out with a mere piglet, as she called him, wasn't for her simply a perverse and transient kind of slumming. If so he'd better make the most of it. If not he'd better make the most of it. Either way, the prospects for this weekend - she in Southampton, he on duty - were non-existent. Andy sighed and stretched his lazily physical limbs. His copy of *More Joy of Sex* slipped from his left hand and fell over itself on the floor. For a moment he closed his eyes.

The rugby ball caught him hard in the stomach. He reacted instantly, simultaneously cradling the ball and swerving to his feet, but in the same instant Gregory Thornton launched himself from the doorway into a tackle around Andy's knees and brought him crashing onto the bed again. Retrieving the ball, Greg stood back, grinning and triumphant. Andy groaned.

'You stupid fucker, you should be done for damaging police property.'

'Which, the ball or the bed?'

'Me, you donkey. That nearly got me in the goolies.'

'You shouldn't leave them lying around. Put some

clothes on.'

'Shit, you sound just like a fucking policeman.'

'Too bloody right. Better that than a reformed hippie like you.'

Andy, pulling on a pair of old black Levis, laughed half-heartedly. 'Now there's not many people know that. Anyway, you're not supposed to remember my sordid past: it was just that one summer of sex and drugs and rock 'n' roll, okay? Good basic training. Taught me a bit about what makes degenerates tick.'

'Degenerates! I can remember when you'd have choked with contempt over a word like that. So what,' asked Greg, getting he hoped imperceptibly a shade more serious, 'made you change sides?'

It wasn't like that. It was things happening, falling into place. Even while I was getting stoned and carrying on with all those weirdos. Then there was a moment - wasn't it in the spring of '88? - when the Prime Minister was abroad somewhere like Australia, and there was that huge demonstration. I remember seeing it on tv and they said something like: "The protesters were mostly supporters of the IRA and homosexuals." And I thought, that's it. You're either with us, trying to keep society in one piece, or you're with the other lot - terrorists, lefties, poofters, subversives in general. They've all got to be smashed. They're all out to destroy us.'

'It was really that simple?'

'Surprisingly, yes.'

'And that was when little Andy decided to sign up with RAID.'

'Not quite. RAID didn't exist then, or if it did I didn't know about it. I started as an ordinary piglet first, remember, just like the rest of you.'

'Maybe I should have got you in the goolies after all.'

'Why, don't you agree with me?'

'Oh yes I agree with you. It's all bloody inconvenient. I might find it inconvenient that the world insists on going round, but that doesn't mean I'd seriously try and stop it.'

'That's not the point.'

'Of course it's the fucking point. You can have these great generalised targets if you like, but it's the detail that gets in the way.'

'I know that. By the way, are there any cans in that cupboard behind you? Great. Chuck us one and help yourself.' The spurt of warm weak lager as he opened the can caught him on the chin and dribbled onto his chest. 'Shit. But yes, I know all about detail. I'm a member of an elite force, remember.'

'Elite?' Greg choked sarcastically. 'As far as I can see, your elite training has taught you exactly two things.'

'Go on.'

'How to look remarkably like a secret policeman in a crowd, and how to beat the shit out of people without leaving marks for the pathologist.'

Andy grinned involuntarily. 'You're only jealous.'

'I'm not. Morbidly curious, perhaps, but not jealous. In fact I suffer from a misplaced nostalgia for the good old days we never knew, *The Blue Lamp* and all that stuff.'

'But Greg, you dumb donkey, you *know* it was never really like that.'

'No, but at least there might have been a time when you could imagine things were like that.'

'And get yourself murdered while you were day-dreaming. Great. Anyway, I'm doing the inconspicuous community bit tomorrow. Marching with the enemy.'

'For once I'll be glad of my uniform.'

'You should see mine.' Andy flung open he wardrobe door and began to throw clothes onto the bed. 'Leather jacket. I'm actually fond of that. Then these jeans - the oldest and tightest and now the most ripped I could find. And this pink t-shirt. Okay, I got Debbie to dye it. I wasn't going to buy one. But it'll look the part.'

'Amazing. Someone'll pick you up if you're not careful.'

'In which case the second half of my training will come in handy. Won't it?'

For a moment he caught Greg looking at him with horrified admiration. Greg, he knew, liked and almost respected him, but at times Andy had this way of creating

9

careless certainties out of the thin air of prejudice. It was as if he'd heard all about good and evil too early - his father was a vicar in Surrey - and had decided that they complicate matters unnecessarily. By way of compensation, his amoral pragmatism had hardened into a creed more rigid than anything his father could preach.

Andy switched on the television. 'We'd better not miss the big speech,' he said. 'Never know, it might be important.'

'Sounds more like ritual devotion to Big Brother to me.'

'No need to scoff. He's transforming this country. And he's transformed your salary.'

'Yes, yes, I know, but he hasn't done much to transform my peace of mind.'

A news bulletin was burbling to its end, gathering up its desultory bunch of headlines. Latest government figures showed some renewed growth in industrial output, and the Chancellor of the Exchequer had restated his faith in his economic strategy which would continue to guide the country towards greater competitiveness and prosperity. A coup in an obscure newly independent state in southern Africa had been averted after the intervention of friendly foreign powers including, it was thought, members of the SAS. In London, strikes and disruptions had continued to affect public services in a number of boroughs: in the worst affected areas, refuse collection and maintenance of other facilities had ceased completely - a combination of overspending, underfunding, and union intransigence was to blame. The Prime Minister was about to announce a major new initiative on public order and would be speaking to the nation shortly.

Andy produced two more cans of lager from the cupboard and handed one to Greg. 'You'll need it,' he grinned.

'There now follows a Prime Ministerial Broadcast,' said the television in the voice once reserved for royal weddings and funerals.

'During the period of our administration,' he said, 'we have worked ceaselessly and successfully to make Great

Britain a better and a safer place in which to live. We have created, as my Right Honourable Friend the Chancellor of the Exchequer was able to confirm today, a society in which increased productivity has led to increased prosperity for all those who take the trouble to earn it. Our country, with its thriving industrial base supported by an educational system which is at last geared to the demands of the real competitive world, now offers unparalleled opportunities for enterprise and initiative. And our international standing, buttressed by a strong and resolute defence policy, is higher than at any time in recent history.

'But we are not complacent. We know that there are problems still to be tackled. We know that they will demand bold and resolute action. We know that they must be addressed in terms which our people will respect and understand. Above all, we know that our efforts, now as at all times in the past, must be directed towards the protection of those values which we all cherish most deeply: our *families* and our *property*.

'It may seem extraordinary that in some parts of our prosperous and successful country, these two most cherishable things, our families and our property, are under threat. It *is* extraordinary. But there are those within our society - the grumblers and the moaners, the indolent and the immoral, the subversives and the agitators - who would seek to undermine and to destroy those values by which all of us, decent, hard-working people, hope to live. The time has come to curtail their evil power and their destructive influence.

'You know, there is a kind of "freedom" advocated by such people which can only be achieved by destroying the very *real* freedoms which you and I enjoy. Their "freedom" is the freedom of the robber to help himself at the bank, of the terrorist to maim and murder elected politicians, of the subversive to indoctrinate your children at school, of the pornographer to peddle filth in the name of art, of the anarchist to parade on the streets, in the press, or on our television screens. And it must be stopped.

'That is why I am speaking to you this evening. To

11

protect our own precious, decent freedoms, it may sometimes be necessary to curtail the so-called freedom of others. We therefore propose to reinforce our existing powers in three ways. Firstly, from this coming Monday, the provisions of the Prevention of Terrorism Act, as amended last year, shall apply to members of all known subversive organisations. Secondly, and from the same date, all public meetings and demonstrations shall in future require a licence obtained in advance from the Home Office, as provided for in the new Public Order Act. And thirdly, the remit of the Media Advisory Council shall be strengthened to provide a more effective check on broadcast and published material. The Home Secretary will be announcing more details of this in Parliament in due course.

'None of these measures will directly affect the lives of decent, law-abiding citizens like you and I. But they will enable the police and the security forces to control more effectively the misguided attempts of society's enemies to undermine our British way of life. We are confident that they will receive your overwhelming support and co-operation.

'God bless you, and goodnight.' The image faded on his fixed, hard smile.

Greg flicked he television off. 'Satisfied?' he asked.

'Nothing there we didn't know already.'

'Perhaps not. But remember I don't have the advantage of your security briefings.'

'Oh come on. It's all harmless stuff.'

'Is it? Then what's it really all about?'

'Warning shots, that's all. Makes it easier for us to nick suspicious characters. Makes it easier for us to keep tabs on suspicious characters we can't nick. Makes suspicious characters think twice before doing things they might get nicked for. If you don't approve of that, you shouldn't be a fucking policeman.'

'I didn't say I disapproved of that. What I disapprove of is, well, the style.'

'Okay, okay, there's all that political edge. He's keeping

the voters happy when they might have forgotten about him in the summer, warming up the issues for the party conference and the autumn by-elections. But they love it. And anyway, we're all involved in politics now. Politics and pornography.'

'Bit unsubtle, with that march tomorrow, all the same.'

'Is it?' Andy grinned.

'You see, your briefings do tell you things I don't know.'

'Of course. But seriously, it puts us in the right if there is any aggro. And it does something for the weekend headlines. "Gay Protest March over Public Order Act" gets upstaged by "PM's New Warning on Public Order." Neat. It's simply a matter of timing. It always is.'

'And what's your role in tomorrow's entertainment?'

'Tomorrow? Observation. Find out who, what, where. Maybe pick up a few leads to follow up next week.'

'Well, it all sounds a bit more than shady to me. I'm not sure that policemen should go round behaving as if they're a mixture of MI5 and SAS with a dash of the Mafia thrown in.'

'That's not a bad job description. Maybe we'll use it one day.'

Andy was amused, and a little irritated, by Greg's lapses into homely moralising. They'd known each other a long time: they shared the same suburban background, though Greg was a year or so older than him. Then they'd diverged. Greg had taken a degree in Sports Studies and English - an odd combination which accurately reflected the imperfectly reconciled halves of his character - before joining the regular force: he was well on his way to a comfortable career, ultimately desk-bound and almost academic, in the CID. Andy meanwhile had spent a wild last year at school which wrecked his chances of a university place: for him, a police career had seemed both an appropriate vehicle for his sporadic energy and a means of escaping the more studious kinds of competitiveness favoured by his brighter contemporaries. The chance of training for RAID, the euphemistically-named Research and Information Department, had appeared after only a few short months on the beat in Croydon. There he thought he'd found the right outlet for his blend of agility with bravado, cunning with recklessness. Now, with a rank and salary above Greg's, he felt able to patronise gently the friend whom he'd once looked up to at their comprehensive.

Greg's posting to the same South West London territory had been at Andy's suggestion. He didn't regret it - there was the chance that sooner or later he could push something interesting in Greg's direction which would help him on his way into the CID, and anyway it was good to have an old drinking partner around - but it created minor problems, all the same. There were things he really couldn't tell Greg, rare nuggets of classified information he picked up at RAID headquarters, and other things which would offend his surprisingly delicate conscience, like the way they sometimes had to treat suspects down at their Hammersmith base - the Hammer Horror they laughingly called it. Even the address of the place, a converted warehouse with the name of a defunct grocery firm proudly displayed on it, wasn't to be revealed to uniformed boys below the rank of Chief Inspector. A further point he couldn't share with Greg was his current vague sense of disappointment: he'd reckoned to be busting the IRA, or at least an international drugs or pornography racket, by now, but instead they had him running about checking up on a bunch of poofters.

Greg seemed, astutely or coincidentally, to read that thought. 'Why did they choose you for this piece of institutionalised queer-bashing?'

Andy ignored the challenge to further self-justification. 'Because,' he said, flexing his muscles, 'I'm a very pretty policeman. And I'm thirsty. Come on, I'll put on a t-shirt that isn't pink, and I'll buy you a beer.'

* * *

The old man was almost certainly dying, Kieran thought. So, probably, was Kieran. He was washing up, an occupa-

14

tion he rather oddly enjoyed, staring partly at the small walled garden with its fuschias and geraniums fading gently into dusk outside the kitchen window and partly at his own image reflected within it. The old man, Bertram Philpotts, stood behind him, alternately drying on a floral tea-towel the objects which Kieran dredged from the lemony suds and running his finger-tips over the boy's shoulders and back. Occasionally their reflected eyes met in the window, and they exchanged sad ironic smiles. They said nothing. In another room, a disc of a late Beethoven quartet was playing.

Despite the dark promise of his name, Kieran Radford was blond. He was twenty-four but had more or less retained his boyish figure and looks through a fortuitous combination of malnutrition and cosmetics. At seventeen, he'd hitched a lift from Liverpool to London; within a month, he was living with a disc-jockey and modelling for *Vulcan*; a year later, he was beginning a long and intermittent affair with an ambitious Labour MP. Since then, he hadn't looked back. He'd cruised culturally up-market, trading his accent for classless urbanity and creating a web of famous friend and lovers, each of whom seemed to deposit some slight sheen of his own reality upon Kieran's unreal, shifting soul. Consequently he now seemed - in the right light, even to himself - unusually well-informed and cultivated, a bright young intellectual with connections, as long as no-one delved too deeply into what he actually did or who he actually was. Today, for instance, he'd slept until lunchtime, cadged a couple of drinks, wandered round the National Gallery, and eventually taken a tube to Earl's Court where in Bertram's flat he cooked with Bertram's ingredients an excellent recipe borrowed from Clive Greenslade. Late tomorrow morning he'd rise from Bertram's bed and shyly ask for a loan to see him through until his next casual job or dole cheque. On such occasions Kieran was plausible enough to convince himself that it was really a loan. He wasn't rent.

'That's the lot,' he said, conjuring a saucepan from the sink. 'Oh no it's not: God's lid,' he added. It was a vague

15

Shakespearian joke he'd picked up somewhere. 'Now that really is the lot.'

'Thank you my dear,' said Bertram, cursorily dabbing the lid. 'Now shall we...?' The gesture wafted towards a second bottle of wine.

'Of course. If you think so, that is.'

The empty forms of civility came easily to him. Besides, one of the few immutable truths about Kieran was his fondness for wine, especially claret, and very especially claret as good as Bertram's Chateau Potensac '82. There was, however, no telling how the second bottle would affect the old man. Bertram Philpotts had until his retirement been head of a small literary publishing house: now, his after-dinner mellowness might equally resolve into literary anecdotage or into a taste for pornographic videos, of which he had an apparently inexhaustible supply. Sometimes, indeed, the two disconcertingly overlapped. 'Something about that boy reminds me of young Joe Ackerley,' he'd suddenly say, and it was hard to know on which level to respond.

Bertram sank heavily onto the sofa. 'I gather the old bitch was making some great speech on the television this evening,' he said. 'Thank god we missed him. I expect he announced that all queers were to be rounded up and exiled to the Falklands.'

'That would be a tight squeeze. It sounds quite promising.'

'It's all very well for us to joke about it, my dear, but I wouldn't want to be your age. They've got it in for you. You really must be careful.'

Kieran, lighting a Gaulloise, gave a quick choking laugh. 'Oh, don't worry about me. I'm indestructible.'

'So you've said before, and as I've said before it isn't true. You could only be indestructible if there was really nothing in there to destroy, and even you've got a mean little soul somewhere.'

'Maybe. Most of the time I feel I'm just a husk. A husk in search of a hunk.'

'Well, there I can't altogether oblige. However, you're a

very lovable husk. Now put another disc on, pour us some more wine, and come over here.'

'What would you like?'

'Anything but that bloody Shostakovich. It upsets me.'

'Right. How about Sergei?'

'Perfect. The second symphony would be ideal. Then we'll be drunk in time for the third movement.'

The music began, Rachmaninov's motto theme unravelling in its huge wave-like gestures through the slow introduction.

'It's marvellous,' said Kieran.

'It's very true and very cruel, full of great spacious gestures which end in little empty rooms. Let's have some wine.'

Kieran poured the wine, and sat down on the sofa beside him.

'I was thinking for some reason about William Brannigan. Have you ever read him?'

'No. Ought I to have done?'

'Not particularly. He was a good minor poet and a bad minor novelist; we started to publish him in the late thirties. Anyway, he was immovably established on the list when I joined the firm after the war. What he was really best at was loathing. He especially loathed George Orwell, though I suspect he simply used Orwell as an emblem for some kinds - most kinds - of writer.'

'Why? I mean, why did he loathe him?'

'Bill couldn't stand the way in which Orwell perpetually wrote articles for left-wing magazines about the awfulness of the world and yet depended on just that awfulness for his bread and butter. He thought Orwell the perfect example of the pseudo-utopian whose utopia would in fact make him very unhappy - if only because there'd be so much less to grumble enjoyably about. I think that oversimplified Orwell a good deal, but basically he had a point.

'Anyway, we were in the French in Dean Street one lunchtime, nineteen fifty-ish I suppose, with some rather excitable arty people. Orwell *wasn't* there, at least. He'd

17

just died. And for some reason Bill became even crosser than usual. It was one of those tiresome conversations about whether the time was good for art or life (it might just as well have been drinking or sex). Suddenly Bill slammed his fist on the table as hard as he could - everyone's glass jumped and at least one shattered - and shouted: "There are *no* good times or bad times. The bad times *are* the good times. The only thing that makes anyone do anything useful is the bloody hideousness of being alive. In a good time you'd all be permanently drunk or asleep. No paintings, no music, no poems, just sheer boring inertia." Something like that, anyway.'

'And you were thinking...?'

'Yes, I was wondering whether he'd have said the same thing today.'

'Perhaps not.'

'Rationally you may be right, but I think he would have done. He was an extremely obstinate man.'

'What happened to him?'

'As a writer or as a human being?'

'Both.'

'As a writer he stopped producing anything publishable. The poems are good, but he hardly wrote any after the war: still, someone should put an edition together - those people in Manchester perhaps. The novels got worse, until eventually I had to turn one down. It was a literary satire about a hypocritical left-wing writer who turned out to be a puppet of the CIA or something. In a way it was quite perceptive when you come to think of what happened to *Encounter* a few years later. But the writer was so obviously and cloddishly modelled on Orwell that I couldn't possibly publish it. Sonia would have sued, and someone from Seckers would have lobbed a brick through our window. They were just round the corner from us, in Carlisle Street. I wrote him an extremely kind letter, and met him for a drink to talk the thing over - I thought that if we bought him lunch at that point he'd probably hurl it at me. The awful thing was that he didn't lose his famous temper at all. He just said, very quietly, "My dear Bertram,

18

you're quite right. The book's a load of shit, and I'm finished." And he was.'

'But he can't have simply vanished into thin air after that.'

'No, he disappeared rather gradually, like the Cheshire cat. He inherited a house somewhere slightly ridiculous, like Tunbridge Wells, and moved out of London. I saw him distantly, with diminishing frequency, whenever he could afford a cheap day return I suppose. Then eventually he faded away completely. I expect he became a monk or a lighthouse keeper. He may well be dead by now, though no-one seems to know for sure. At least, the *Times* hasn't used my obituary of him yet.'

'That can't have been easy to write.'

'Strangely enough it wasn't difficult. If he'd been wandering around here now, drinking huge gins and writing terrible books, there would have been a problem. But his best work was distanced and so was he; I could turn him into a character.'

'Does that mean he wasn't a character until you turned him into one?'

'Not at all. He was well on the way to turning himself into a character, even when I knew him. If you'd pumped him up a bit and given him a handlebar moustache, he'd have made a very good Jimmy Edwards figure - a sort of consciously absurd retired colonel type. It was always as if he needed to be a slightly bigger man than he actually was. The rest of him didn't quite match the scale of his loathing. But he was certainly a character.'

'You must let me read his poems sometime.'

'Perhaps I will. You know my dear, I'm beginning to feel rather possessive about the past. I'm afraid of the ways in which it might be damaged by the present, as if the present is so poisonous that it can reach even what seemed complete and concluded. That's really what I meant when I said I wondered what Bill would make of it all. I'm not sure that even his loathing would be equal to the task.'

Kieran didn't reply. Instead he looked aimlessly around the room which he now knew so well - better, in a sense, than Bertram, who had lived here so long that he scarcely seemed to notice the place any more. The room was part of the past about which Bertram felt so possessive, a past in which books were permanent artefacts with proper bindings which sat squarely on their solid mahogany shelves. They had faded with sunlight and clogged with generations of London dust but they retained their coherence and integrity. They weren't flimsy and temporary, like Kieran's one publication, a stapled small-press pamphlet, or like Kieran. Bertram had scarcely bought anything, except wine, for a dozen years. The video recorder and CD player were the only representatives of the present - brash, black, and Japanese - in the room. Kieran refilled Bertram's glass and helped himself to more wine. The third movement began.

Here, for a little while, the empty rooms of which Bertram had spoken opened out into an enormous darkly-lit seascape. Not that it was altogether reassuring: the colours were vivid and stormy, the waves rolled in with overwhelmingly muscular power. The brass thundered ominously. But calm of a kind returned as the strings once again recalled the opening clarinet theme. A particularly idiotic boy whom Kieran had taken home to his own bedsit in Brixton had once said that it sounded like an Acker Bilk record.

With one arm already round his shoulders, Bertram began with his free hand fumblingly to unbutton Kieran's shirt. Kieran smiled: he too felt affectionate and slightly drunk. They both knew nothing would come of it.

* * *

'But you've never been on a football pitch in your life,' said Bill. 'At least, not willingly.'

'Exactly,' said Jeremy, 'that's exactly what I'm getting at. It's the question of what triggers the imagination to put you totally, not just as it were speculatively, in a place you've never been or wished to be, and in a time before you were born. I was there, and surprised to be there. It

20

wasn't as if I was creating the thing as I went along.'

'You were no more than an interested observer. The creative voyeur. As usual.'

'Well, you may be right there, but I'm still intrigued. There I was, sitting on the sea wall, and I dozed off for maybe a couple of minutes. First I was on this football pitch, and the immediately strange thing was that the players all wore those very long shorts and had that sort of pre-war look about them. Anyway, I walked calmly off the pitch and into a street, behind a woman wearing a hat, again certainly not the kind of hat I've seen anyone wearing in my lifetime. And then, prompted by that I suppose, I turned to look at a shop window, and it was full of those hats on little chromium-plated stands. Now that isn't even a kind of shop that's existed for twenty or thirty years. And yet, even though it was all unexpected, it was somehow coherent, almost more real than standing here now.'

'Did you kick a football?'

'No.'

'Did you buy a hat?'

'Of course not.'

'That proves it.' Bill didn't say what it proved. 'Let's have another drink.'

'Last orders,' shouted Ken, and clanged a bell. He was used to these conversations. 'A large gin and tonic and a pint of Broadside?'

'I'll get them,' said Jeremy. Bill didn't disagree.

As he paid for the drinks, Jeremy smiled optimistically along the bar at a boy who looked more like a Californian surfer than a Suffolk fisherman. The boy, since this wasn't London, grinned and waved before turning back to his girlfriend.

Bill noted the exchange of gestures. 'I'll say one thing for you queers,' he remarked kindly, 'you live in hopes. On the whole, I rather approve of that. After you've had a drink or two, you completely discount the possibility that you could be anything other than young and beautiful yourself. How old are you, anyway?'

21

'Forty-three.'

'Well I'm seventy-nine next month. I don't see what that has to do with anything, but still. Perhaps it's time you stopped thinking about boys and got on with the great book. Unless you can do both. What the hell are you going to do with the rest of your life?'

Jeremy laughed. 'Actually, I'm really quite happy with things - that is, until people like you start bullying me. I've got enough part-time teaching to pay the bills, enough writing to stop my brain seizing up completely, and enough alcohol and sea air to sleep well at night.'

As if at the mention of sea air, the hairy cream-coloured retriever at Jeremy's feet looked up and uttered a long yawning sigh.

'Okay. Ben reckons it's closing time. If I had a pub, I'd train him to bark last orders.'

'Well,' said Bill, 'keep an eye on that sea. If you live here until you're as old as I am, you'll probably be under it.'

'Yes, I know, the greenhouse effect. I don't think I'll mind too much if it just gradually creeps up on us: we'd adjust as we went along, build bigger walls, have bigger sandbags. But I don't at all like the idea of a sudden great storm and flood. Were you here in '53?'

'No, I turned up here a few years after that, but there were still people about who'd lost everything. Of course, they were used to loss then: it wasn't that long after the war. If it all happened again now, it would seem much worse: apart from the odd hurricane, most English people under fifty have very little conception of what physical destruction is like in their own country.'

'It's a long time, all the same. I mean, that you've been here. You must like it.'

'Yes, on the whole I do. I'd lived the mad metropolitan literary life for long enough.'

'Can I ask you something? It's just a thought.'

'It's not like you to prevaricate.'

'Okay, it's just that I've been asked to do a piece about living outside London - or, more precisely, about what it's like for a writer to leave London and adjust to a different lifestyle. That sounds a bit kitsch, but you know what I mean. I was wondering if we could chat about it sometime, or perhaps I could tape an interview with you.'

Bill let out a hoot, or it may have been a howl, of laughter. 'I do hope you're not going to try and rediscover me. That *would* be a waste of time. Mind you, I could do with some royalties. Apart from that, I don't think I want to be rediscovered, and I don't think anyone would be in the slightest degree interested in me. But I don't mind talking to you or to a tape recorder, as long as you provide the booze.'

'It's a deal. And now I'd better give Ben his dose of sea air. I assume you're going in the opposite direction.'

'Yes, uphill to anonymity.'

'Well, I'll see you tomorrow probably, and we'll fix a time for that chat. You could always wear a false beard for the recording.'

Ben was already at the door, so Jeremy followed him. There was no sign of the surfer-fisherman and his girl.

The rain had cleared away. Jeremy walked to the coastguard station and looked south along the shore. There were lights out at sea, and to their right a sequence of red dots above Orford Ness which he took to be navigation lights for Woodbridge airfield. Below and to his left the sea lapped unobtrusively against the stony beach. Ben frolicked off down there in a sudden burst of frivolous energy, and soon he could just be made out dispassionately inspecting a fish-head. It was after closing time on a summer Friday and yet here, at the edge of England, there was still something like peace.

It had been a good evening: at best as well as at worst, Jeremy even now thought of himself as an exile, and he responded with the exile's exaggerated sensitivity to gestures of acceptance or rebuff. He had been quietly amused by Clive's vaguely apocalyptic phone-call; he had written a bit; and he had ended up, as usual, in the pub at the unfashionable end of town where the exile felt most at home. These days, even in summer, most of the drinkers were more or less permanent inhabitants: a lot of casual

23

tourists had been scared off by Sizewell, although there remained a sprinkling of regular visitors, second-home owners and habitual flat-renters who continued to return with a defiant loyalty which was mildly endearing. Apart from them, there was the odd social mix which had, after all, persuaded Jeremy to settle here: fishermen and craftsmen, musicians and writers, unconventional yachtsmen who'd quarrelled with the other, smarter pubs. He felt at home in a community of anachronisms.

And there was the sea. He'd always felt drawn to it, not in a prissy watercolourist way but on account of its sheer physical implacability. It wasn't there for easy reassurance: it made things better simply by its monstrous indifference to their trivial demands. One day, no doubt soon, the tawdry business of human politics would find a way of irrevocably messing up the sea, but that hadn't quite happened yet. Meanwhile, it could still perform some pretty impressive tricks. Tonight, for instance, a huge orange moon near the horizon had spread an amber ladder across the water towards him. A stairway to the stars. Jeremy grinned at the sentimentality of the pop-song image, and then thought: No, it's the fear of what we call sentimentality that's itself dishonest, sentimental. After all, all this is true.

TWO

Kieran would of course have preferred to meet in a gay bar, but Clive had as usual stipulated the Lamb and Flag. Clive, he knew, didn't care for and sometimes vehemently disapproved of the gay scene, except for odd evenings after a few drinks when suddenly he got to like it very much indeed. But this time - twelve noon on a sunlit Saturday, pleasantly cool and unoppressive for August - he was probably right. The gay pubs would be packed solid with people like them going on the march against the new Public Order Act, and anyway, he'd say, what was the point of preaching to the converted? The escalators at Leicester Square would probably be out of order, so Kieran went on a stop and chanced his luck with the lifts at Covent Garden. He fought his way out of the station and walked down Long Acre, idly trying to identify the potential marchers, but the crowd was mostly the moneyed, stylish lot which colonised London on a summer weekend, and the prettiest ones were probably just innocent tourists. He risked a deliberate near-collision with a couple of German boys, then slipped through Conduit Court and into Rose Street. Clive, pathologically punctual as ever, was standing outside the Lamb with a pint in his hand. Seeing Kieran, he put his glass on the ledge, stepped forward, embraced and kissed him.

'Well,' said Kieran, grinning. 'That wasn't like you.'

'What wasn't?'

'Kissing in public, in broad daylight, outside a straight pub. Two of those I'd have believed, but not all three at once.'

'Oh,' said Clive, almost sheepish. 'I'm just getting into the spirit of the occasion. Let's get you a drink. Meanwhile, guard mine.' He vanished into the darkness of the pub.

Kieran glanced round at the packed narrow street. The

old looked much as they always had done, but the young had suddenly, this summer, got much younger. He felt a small familiar panic: it wasn't simply that he was becoming older himself, it was that he found himself increasingly adrift in a strange ageless bubble. He shut out the thought by quietly whistling a fragment of Mahler while continuing to look aimlessly about him.

'Any doughnuts?' Clive had reappeared, carrying a second pint.

'A couple, down by the railings.'

'Oh yes, not bad.' They both laughed. Doughnuts: it was an old joke from a play, *Sinners and Saints*, which they'd seen together three or four years ago, soon after they'd first met. Anything fanciable in a t-shirt and tight jeans was a doughnut: the difficulty lay in choosing between the superficial, sugary ring ones and the substantial ones with jam inside. Kieran had once been an indisputable doughnut himself; now he wasn't so sure.

'Odd, thinking of that today.'

'Why?'

'Remember how we came to see that play?'

'Oh yes, it all started with that other march.' It had been the day of the Stop the Clause march in the spring of '88. On the Embankment a girl had pressed a leaflet into Clive's hand: it advertised some play or other, and Clive had simply folded and pocketed it. Some time later, they'd looked at it properly. 'Good grief, it's Tim,' Clive had said. 'He's a marvellous actor I used to know. We must see it.' And he had been marvellous. Kieran had liked him when they'd met for a drink after the performance, had wanted to see him again.

'Things seemed easier then,' said Clive. 'I mean, there was Anderton, but he was a joke. There were people getting ill, but we didn't actually know anyone who'd died. There was Clause 28, but it seemed to be bringing us together. There wasn't this insistent mind-numbing pressure I feel everywhere today.'

'You mean we were both younger.'

'Probably.' He laughed. 'Okay, *obviously*. Though in

26

fact I don't feel at all paranoid here. I think it's because this pub, and bits of Covent Garden, and what's left of literary Soho, were places I'd made my own very early on. They can't take them away from me now. That's why I'm never really at ease in most of the gay bars: they're so tacky and transitory, and I want things to be better than that.'

'I know,' said Kieran. He really did know. It was a feeling to which Clive could easily persuade him and which he would then quite genuinely believe. He too wanted, when his extended playtime was over, to write the great book, to be taken seriously by some better posterity. He smiled ruefully and said, 'But we are tacky and transitory, my dear.'

'Yes, yes, I know. What did you do last night?'

'Oh, went round to Philpotts. Cooked the old sweetie a meal - one of your recipes, of course, and not up to your standard - then drank some more of his wine and listened to him talk. That was it really. He's preoccupied with an obscure writer he once published called William Brannigan, who seems to have vanished off the face of the earth without actually dying. Bertram seems to think I should track him done and write a book - *In Search of Brannigan* or something. He's always coming up with great projects to save my soul.'

'It's a thought. I've heard of him. He's probably an ancient recluse living in a lighthouse or something.'

'That's almost exactly what Bertram said.'

'It's almost exactly what I've heard.'

'Well, perhaps I'll give it a try, sooner or later. Good god.'

'What's the matter?'

'Oh nothing. One of those two doughnuts, the one in the stripey red T-shirt: I've just realised where I've seen him before. He's a friend of Martin's. They were in the Pit together the other night.'

Clive smiled, but looked very slightly pained. 'Is there anyone you don't know?'

'Oh I wouldn't say I know him. Just one of those things.'

Simultaneously, and to the mild astonishment of the drinkers nearest to them, they burst into song for half a verse or so.

'We should grab something to eat. It's a longish trek to Kennington Park.' The march, in homage or in mourning, was to retrace the route of April '88.

'Unless we cheat, like last time. Tag on towards the end, then nip over Westminster Bridge, along the Albert Embankment, and catch up with the prettiest ones.'

'Yes, that *was* a good idea, wasn't it. Either way, I'm going to get a ploughman's. They still do real Blue Shropshire here. Do you want one?'

'No, I'll get a burger in the Strand.'

'You always were incredibly vulgar. Be good till I get back.'

'Of course.' Kieran stood against the railings and looked upwards, beyond the gravity-defying plants which toppled in crazy profusion, this as every summer, from the pub's first-floor window-boxes, towards the deep blue sky and wispy impatient clouds, framed into a vivid irregular shape by the tops of the buildings: it was like the fragment of sky you could never fit into a jigsaw. As a child he'd sought the loneliness of empty spaces, spending days, whole summers it seemed, walking on the moors. Now he sought, and had found, the stranger loneliness of the city.

He glanced again in the direction of the stripey doughnut, whom he'd known a little more closely than he'd admitted to Clive, even though he couldn't remember his name - Justin or Jason or something. He'd quarrelled with Martin over that one - they'd quarrelled over most things - towards the end of their long if patchy relationship. For a politician, Martin had been absurdly naive about the politics of human affairs, by turns over-generous, over-protective, and childishly jealous. Shortly after Justin or Jason had moved in with Martin, Kieran had slept with him, a long wild midsummer night's fuck high on wine and dope, and subsequently hadn't bothered to conceal the fact from Martin. And soon after that, Justin or Jason had moved out again: Kieran had been marginally

28

surprised to see him with Martin in a bar a few days earlier, but that was so often the way. Now he tried to catch his eye, and succeeded, only to be rewarded with a quick sneering smile which fell seriously short of friendly acknowledgement. That, too, was so often the way.

Clive returned, carrying a plate on which reposed, along with bread and butter and pickles, a large wedge of the garish orange and blue cheese which he found so inexplicably attractive. He had the smug look of one who has just been chatting up a barman. But it soon faded. 'Panic and emptiness,' he said.

'Why?' asked Kieran, wondering if he'd caught the exchange of looks with the stripey doughnut.

'Oh London, London. I can never quite avoid those pangs of despair these days.'

'My dear, you thrive on your pangs. You wouldn't know what to do without them.'

Clive attacked the cheese with mournful satisfaction. 'Yes, I suppose so. But these days I want solid things about me. Things that are real.' He laughed. 'Poor bloody poets. Both of us.'

Justin or Jason ambled away, an arm round his friend's shoulders, past where Moss Bros used to be.

'Presumably,' said Clive between mouthfuls, 'your MP will seize the opportunity for a party political when we all get to Kennington.'

'He's not my MP. In any sense. He's far too famous even for me to know these days. Anyway, we don't have to stay and listen to him.'

'That's true. I'm actually not particularly keen on public figures standing up and talking about solidarity. It's the unnerving impression of a dummy abruptly coming to life. Apart from which, their motives *must* be suspect.'

'Generally yes. But there surely aren't going to be many votes in gay rights these days.'

'There will be in Kennington Park.'

Kieran laughed. 'Not his constituency. Anyway, he'll probably concentrate on demolishing the PM's broadcast yesterday.'

29

'Which neither of us saw.'

'No, thank god. Do you know what he said?'

'The usual sort of stuff. Freedom and prosperity for everyone with a family, a mortgage and a company car, and the rest of us had better shut up.'

'Oh, is that all.'

'Not quite. And this bloody Public Order Act will be in force from Monday, after which all marches and demonstrations will need some sort of licence from the government.'

'So this really will be the last.'

'Yes, save the last march for me.'

'Well, we'd better get on with it then.'

They walked down Bedford Street to the Strand. Here the crowd was beginning to change its consistency, much of it moving purposefully towards Villiers Street, and a van-load of riot police were lingering without any attempt at concealment, waiting for something to happen. So too were a bunch of neo-nazi skinheads from the New Britain Campaign, edging their way from among the drunkards and derelicts sprawled in Chandos Place. The trouble was, one or two of them were bearably attractive.

'I could almost go for that one on the right,' said Kieran, not quite out of earshot.

'But you don't like pain. Remember? More's the pity,' Clive added, almost to himself.

'Oh all right. I'm going across to Macdonald's to get a burger. What are you going to do? I know you wouldn't be seen dead in there.'

'I'll be in the Music Discount Centre, among the CDs. Somewhere in the region of the letter T.'

Kieran crossed the street and fought his way to the counter in Macdonald's where his burger was dispatched by a dough-faced girl. He ate most of it while being jostled on the pavement, and finished it off on a surprisingly unpopulated traffic island. He wasn't entirely sure about today. Gay politics generally left him at best unmoved, as a time-wasting occupation pursued by the determinedly miserable, but the idea of walking along the Embankment in the sunshine surrounded by boys seemed pleasant enough. He was buggered if he was going to listen to any speeches at the end of it, though. Least of all from Martin fucking Baxter.

He found Clive, as he'd anticipated, contemplating rival versions of *A Child of our Time*.

'Next week,' said Clive.

'But you've already got it.'

'Yes, I know, but on LP and scratched. And it is so incredible. Which recording?'

'Previn,' said Kieran, without hesitation. 'It's much the best. Apart from which, it's got that stunning photograph of Herschel Grynspan on it.'

'Right. What happened to the burger?'

'Scoffed it.'

'That was bloody quick. Piglet.'

'Oink. Dogsty.'

They both laughed. They'd invented the animal game one afternoon when, driving through a particularly bucolic piece of East Anglia, they'd been obstructed by a barely-moving horse-box pulled by a Land-Rover. 'I reckon its paws are sticking out the bottom and it's pushing the Land-Rover,' Clive had said. 'But horses don't have paws, dear.' 'Okay then, cat-box.' 'Horse's whiskers.' 'Cat-chestnut.' 'Horsealogue.' It normally started with something basic, like horse/cat or pig/dog, and progressed to more exotic species later on.

'Pig-kennel.'

'Doghead.'

They crossed the Strand and squeezed into Villiers Street, which was now almost completely blocked with people.

'Talking of which,' said Clive, 'there are a few of them about.'

'What?'

'Pigs. Or dogs.'

'Swarms. No, herds, packs. Dog-herds, pig-packs. We must stop this.' They'd bumped into each other, and into several other people, and were now supporting each other,

31

arms round each other's shoulders, like a pair of hysterical drunkards. Kieran was in fact glad that Clive had loosened into this mildly anarchic mood. There'd been that moment, back at the Lamb and Flag, when he'd seemed on the point of withdrawing into some inner despair: and with Clive, as Kieran knew all too well, withdrawal was for once the exact term. He'd suddenly disappear inside himself, evidently as unable to get out as anyone else was to get in, and the only thing to do then was to wait for his eventual emergence. It could be minutes, hours, days. He wasn't an easy man to love, though at best that probably made him more lovable than he himself knew.

On the steps up to Charing Cross Station, a man was standing on his head playing the harmonica, but no-one was taking any notice of him.

'We're never going to get down there,' said Kieran. 'At least, not if we want to squeeze past the crowds.'

'We could try that street on the other side of the station. What's it called? Craven Street?'

'Could do.' They both stared at the upturned harmonica player, as if expecting him to advise them. 'Though it'll be just the same. And the fascists went that way.'

'I thought you fancied one of them.'

'I don't fancy being cornered by the lot of them in Craven Street. Let's push on.'

By keeping close to the buildings it proved unexpectedly easy to slide past the marchers, who were already instinctively gathering into a central procession. Turning the corner by Embankment tube, Kieran almost collided with a blond boy in a leather jacket: the boy looked at him, and at Clive, with obvious interest or recognition, though Kieran didn't remember the face. He would have remembered it, of that much he was certain.

The crowd was at its densest here, impeded by policemen and sellers of *Socialist Worker* moving among it, but they finally emerged into the relative spaciousness of Northumberland Avenue. One of the uglier skinheads, badly cut about the face and with his hands bloody, was being dragged from Craven Street by four uniformed

32

police towards a waiting van. The boy in the leather jacket scurried past, this time heading towards Westminster Bridge.

* * *

Easing his way through the crowd, Andy thought of other things he could be doing on a sunny Saturday afternoon. Playing cricket. Drinking on the green outside his local in Surrey. Fucking Debbie. Debbie. She'd started to go wild lately, she wanted him to do things which made him worry not only about her but about himself. He must remember to return those handcuffs to the office. And after all that, or rather simultaneously, so that it seemed to be part of the same wildness, she'd be asking him to take her to plays, concerts, ballet even. There was something wrong there.

There was something wrong here too. Careful though he'd been in perfecting his image for the occasion, an altogether more queenly preparation than he dared admit, Andy hadn't known quite what to expect when he arrived. His preconceptions had oscillated between a dour, angry parade, like the miners' rally he and his colleagues had so joyfully sabotaged a few months earlier, and a hysterically camp, not to say pornographic, extravaganza with plenty of arrests for infringements of public decency. In the event, apart from one little incident he'd needed not to see, he was confronted with a kind of controlled carnival - a mass of various and rather cheerful people behaving a great deal better than your average football crowd. They were still poofters, of course. But in their very refusal to offend him in the superficial ways which he could comprehend, they offended him very deeply indeed.

Andy knew what he thought about homosexuals, and he at least had wit enough to see that what he thought didn't entirely add up. On one level, they were a source of harmless merriment, the stuff of sitcoms and pub jokes. Until Aids, their humorous potential had been imbued with a ludicrous innocence, though these days the jokes had a darker and more daring edge, like those about damaged

33

Pakistanis or half-witted American politicians. On another level, there was a clear distinction between sexual playfulness and sexual interest: it was one thing for a guy to make a grab for your dick in the changing-room after a match, quite another if you suspected he might seriously enjoy handling it. Last season there'd been one, a tough and wiry scrum-half, who'd let something slip - it was no more than a discreet, veiled enquiry about Andy's sexuality, but it was enough. When the rest of the team heard about it, they put cherries in his lager, shaving-foam in his tea, and poured purple paint over his car. Andy had heard he was now training to be an actor.

As far as Aids was concerned, Andy was fairly rational: education and training had done their stuff. He certainly didn't share the view, virulently expressed by a journalist in the tabloid press that morning, that the procession consisted of an infected, contagious army bent on spreading its plague throughout the population. He knew that in relative terms the disease was on the decrease among the homosexual population, on the increase among heterosexuals. He didn't regard homosexuals as inherently unhealthy or unclean. He simply loathed hem intuitively as an absurdity, an indignity, a self-humiliating spectacle only worthy of further humiliation.

Andy had found himself a vantage-point on the Victoria Embankment towards Westminster Bridge, from which he could view the procession as it passed. At the head of it were two surprisingly famous pop singers, a soap-opera actor, and Martin Baxter MP. He was the pinko poofter they had, eventually, to nail. It was political, sure, but that didn't particularly worry Andy. As opposition front bench spokesman on home affairs, Baxter had become something more than a nuisance: he was a threat to stability, to good government, and if he ever got into office he'd be a threat to the police and security forces. He'd made speeches attacking the shadowy activities of RAID, pledging to abolish the 'secret police'. Apart from that, there were some difficult by-elections coming up, and someone somewhere in Whitehall wanted a scandal to discredit the

34

opposition. Baxter had won a great deal of respect not only for his integrity and his debating skill but for his openness about his sexuality; still, there were skeletons in his cupboard, and Andy's job was to give them a good rattling.

He sat on the wall and turned for a moment towards the river: there were pleasure-boats, people on them drinking and laughing. Happiness was easy: you just didn't have to try too hard. But as for this lot.... At that moment a pair of cheerful youths pranced up and handed him a pink leaflet headed 'HOW TO FUCK A GOVERNMENT' - except that between the third and fourth words an elevated 'UP' had been added, perched above a cartoon of Big Ben teetering on the point of an erect penis. They skipped away, back into the crowd, leaving Andy to smile grimly at the absurdity of it all. He turned his attention back to the march, to the banners carried by different groups. Every sizeable town, every college or university, and every other house in Amsterdam seemed to have sent a delegation. A group of enchained women carried a placard which said 'VEGETARIAN S/M DYKES' and which ceased to amuse him when he realised that they thought it at least as funny as he did. That was one of the things he couldn't take, the mixture of seriousness and self-parody.

Then he caught sight of a couple he'd noticed earlier, by the tube. He knew all about them. The older one, Clive Greenslade, was a writer and editor heavily involved with subversive publishing: unlike Martin Baxter, he was merely a nuisance, but for Andy his nuisance-value had a personal bite. That magazine he edited - *Pendulum*, it was called - had printed an article about anti-gay attitudes in the police, citing a particularly nasty incident in which Andy had been involved: Greenslade would have to be sorted out, warned off, before he followed it up and started naming names. His friend, Kieran Radford, was apparently a young man with contacts: there was a Baxter connection there too, and Andy wanted to find out more about it. The pair of them were walking on the edge of the procession, evidently intending to slip in and out of it as the fancy took

35

them and perhaps, almost like Andy himself, not quite knowing whether to play the role of participant or observer. He decided to tag along a little behind them, almost certain that Kieran at least registered the move, but that wouldn't necessarily be to his disadvantage. Despite the cacophonous chanting and singing groups, he could just about pick up fragments of their conversation. They seemed to be talking, as homosexuals so obsessively did, about their social arrangements, or disarrangements, for the next few days.

'Monday,' said Kieran, 'I'm going to the theatre with Philpotts - *Troilus and Cressida*, I think - but we might meet for a drink on Tuesday.'

'Early evening?'

'If you like. I ought to get home and do some reading and writing sometime this week, and anyway I shan't have enough money to booze all night.'

'Shit,' said Clive, 'I can't do Tuesday. I've just remembered I'm having dinner with Colin in a vain attempt to get him to write something which meets our deadline.'

'Oh well,' said Kieran: he didn't seem at all put out. 'I expect I'll just wander round to the Pit and see whether anything interesting turns up.' Andy surely didn't imagine the glance and quick grin in his direction over Kieran's shoulder. He smiled back, momentarily using his eyes in a gesture of acknowledgement and complicity which he hadn't known he knew. Clive, distracted by someone on the pavement at whom he was pointing and then waving, had noticed nothing; now, putting his arm round Kieran's shoulders, he steered them both out of the march altogether towards this other friend. Andy walked on: he'd sidle off at Westminster Bridge and consider his next move.

He felt distinctly unsettled, more panicky than he wanted to admit to himself. He knew he was attractive: he liked being looked at, loathed being ignored. But this was different - except that it wasn't, it was disconcertingly ordinary, familiar, instinctive. And then there was the sheer number of them: there must have been literally thousands of men around him who'd find him desirable. It was not that he felt in any danger of being tempted - there was absolutely no chance of *that*; but he was aware of how easy it was to be apparently and mistakenly implicated. He remembered how, when he was quite a young child, there'd been that Tom Robinson song, 'Glad to be Gay'; how seductively contagious its chorus had been; how once, without thinking, he'd heard himself singing along too.

* * *

It had been odd, running into Philip like that. He'd been going somewhere completely else, of course, and had simply stopped to watch the parade go by; but all the same Clive had been glad to claim him as an acquaintance and to claim, a little dishonestly, the march for himself. He'd also, as usual, been quite happy to show off Kieran. They'd chatted for a moment or two in the inconsequential manner of friends meeting in a London street at any other time; then Philip had said 'See you later' and was gone.

They hadn't stayed long at Kennington Park. When they arrived, now very much at the tail-end of the march, a dreadful Scottish punk comedian was all too obviously about to be followed on stage by an even less promising rock band. The air was saturated, as only urban summer air can be, with the smell of burgers and kebabs which seemed gradually to be forming into a visible, sticky haze. There were tents selling warm fizzy beer and undrinkable wine in plastic cups. And there were so many people - some of them vaguely familiar faces from pubs and bars, others so fresh and innocent that this was clearly the one event in their lives - that two defectors could escape unnoticed and with reasonably clear consciences. In any case Clive had wanted to get home by late afternoon to cook, hungrily, a meal that would take some time in the oven.

So, four hours later, in the kitchen at Salisbury Road, a kind of Habitat time-warp with iconoclastic additions, he watched with pleasure as Kieran finished eating. Cooking for Kieran, whose response to food usually managed to be at once rapturous and judicious, was one of life's most simple and ample delights.

'My dear,' said Kieran, smiling in the self-mocking reiteration of an acknowledged formula but not meaning it any the less, 'you have surpassed yourself.'

'Yes,' Clive replied, 'that was pretty bloody marvellous.' It was a dish which he often cooked in his lapses from vegetarianism and one which pleased him partly because of the classic simplicity of its ingredients - beef, garlic, onions, tomatoes, peppers with the inspired additions of ginger at the frying stage and soy sauce in the casserole - and partly because of its humble origin: he had found it in an old Sainsbury's cookery book and with a little tinkering made it his own. Whether he would ever make Kieran his own was another matter: most of the time, he thought he was happy with the occasional, unpossessive nature of their relationship - he knew for certain he couldn't live with someone full-time - but there were moments when he old demon of possessive love sneaked into his mind, and this was one of them. Kieran caught his look and decoded it at once.

'Stop looking like that,' he said kindly, 'and have some more wine.'

'And cheese.'

'And cheese. And biscuits. Those healthy rectangular ones I like, if you've got some.'

Clive pushed the biscuit barrel and the cheese board across the table, and poured more claret into both their glasses.

'Thank you. Lovely wine. Much better than Bertram's yesterday.'

Clive laughed. 'Liar. I know Bertram's famous for his cellar.'

'No, really. I mean, I suppose Bertram's wine may have been "better" in some technical sense, but I'm enjoying this much more. I'm enjoying being here much more.' He put his hand across the table and squeezed Clive's wrist.

'And I'm enjoying you being here.' They both giggled at

the descent into social cliché. 'So what are we going to do this evening?'

Kieran, sculpting cheese onto a biscuit, paused for a moment. 'Not a lot, I don't suppose. Go to the pub, have a few beers, upset some of the locals. Come back, have some coffee, scotch if you've got any, listen to some music, go to bed. It's more than enough as far as I'm concerned.'

'Yes, that's fine. And at some point we'll decide to get up early tomorrow morning and drive into the country.'

'Whereas in fact we'll stay in bed until eleven, have breakfast, and go back to the pub.'

'Precisely.'

'Then that's settled.'

'You know what I think?' said Kieran through a biscuit.

'Probably.'

'I think you need a few more rough boys around the place. I'm too gentle and and cuddlesome for that side of you.'

'You'll do for now. Anyway, the chance would be a fine thing.'

'You should try advertising. Like Julian. He's overrun with them.'

'I don't know why. He's totally objectionable.'

'Well, he advertises. Photography. You've got a camera, after all, you've even got a studio. Anyway, that's what Julian does. They all know it means sex. Did I tell you I stayed at Julian's one night last week?'

'No.' Clive couldn't quite keep the disapproval out of his voice.

'Oh it's all right. I didn't sleep with him. He's got this absurd new boy called Kevin who seems to turn up just about every other day, with an Adidas bag full of gear to dress up in and, of course, to strip off. A couple of weeks ago, he came as a spaceman. It started with a pretence at photography, but mostly he likes being watched, the more the merrier. So I got asked in as a observer. Lovely blond footballer type, rough as they come. But now he's taken to doing it on the balcony. So there we were, the three of us, Julian with his camera, and Kevin doing his stuff above

SW10, and no-one else batting an eyelid.' Kieran paused. 'Still, it does mean that Julian's got the best fed geraniums in London.'

'A window-box in N17 doesn't have quite the same possibilities. But it's all a bit cross-making. Julian's at least in his mid-fifties.'

'He lies about his age. Knocks ten years off. And the strange thing is they don't seem to mind or notice. It *is* like art, after all: suspension of disbelief.'

Clive smiled indulgently: Kieran, it sometimes seemed, lived in a hectic amoral world in which everything was running just a little too fast. He'd envied it, once, had wanted to learn the trick of operating so that your feet so seldom touched the ground. Later, of course, he'd realised that it was all simply a strategy against despair, no better and no worse than his own.

'I'll wash up,' said Kieran. 'I insist.' He would, Clive knew, insist.

'Coffee now or later?'

'Later. I'm going to feel pubbish quite soon. You're the only person I know who's as fond of beer as I am.'

'Okay. I'll dry.'

He watched Kieran begin to attack the sinkful of crockery; beyond him, beyond the kitchen window, dusk was charming the random run-down townscape into deceptive gentleness. Occasionally their reflected eyes met in the window, and they exchanged sad ironic smiles. They went about their tasks in an easy domestic silence born of habit, Kieran as usual addressing himself with enthusiasm to the contents of the two ochre enamelled bowls, once so trendy and now so chipped, while Clive stowed the crockery away in pine-faced cupboards of units whose 'marble' formica tops had begun to flake at the edges, through collisions and usage, leaving oddly improper glimpses of chipboard, like random flashes of flesh caught through holes in a garment. After a while Clive put down the tea-towel and, holding Kieran's shoulders, kissed him very slowly and gently on the back of the neck. Then, as he moved aside, their eyes met once

40

more in the mirror of the kitchen window. Clive grimaced.

'God I'm getting old. Just look at me.'

'You are not getting old, or at any rate you're getting a lot less old than you should be. It's all a matter of poor self-image. That, and an insufficiency of rough boys.'

'Probably. I do dislike being alone these days. It's strange. I'd always been the kind of miserable old sod who likes solitude - I was always relieved when a friend left and I had the place to myself again. Even you, at first. But quite suddenly, a couple of years ago, I started to get terrified, not of loneliness exactly, but of the insecurity that can go with being alone. I suppose that's another sign of age.'

'It's a sign of the times. Anyway, you'll cheer up with a few beers inside you - you'll probably start chatting up some entirely straight boy in your inimitable way.'

'Like that rather pretty Scottish one last time? You remember? The one with the ears.'

'Oh yes, well you'd need something to hold on to.'

'He was very sweet about it. All he said was, "Och, you're way out of order." Probably comes from being a mate of Dylan's. Otherwise he'd have beaten the shit out of me.'

'Which...'

'Which I *wouldn't* have liked. Are you fit?'

'More or less.'

'Right. I'll just put on some sillier jeans and I'll be with you.'

Clive went into the bedroom and took from the wardrobe his favourite pair of tight faded Lee jeans. They and a white t-shirt sort of went with Saturday nights in summer: it was silly, he knew, a middle-aged man dressing down like a rent-boy, but maybe not that silly. As he changed, he admired himself selectively in the bedroom mirror: his bum was still better than he'd seen on many a twenty-year-old, and his cock, though lazy with alcohol most of the time, had its moments of inspiration if with diminishing frequency. Some modest working out had restored his pectorals and biceps to reasonable shape for his age, but there was no excuse for the beer-gut, except beer. He peeled himself into the jeans like a banana in reverse. Meanwhile he could hear Kieran in the bathroom creating with aerosols, bottles, jars and tubes the little medley of sound-effects which habitually preceded his comings and goings - to the pub or to bed. Changing places, they squeezed past each other in the passage, their lips brushing in a passing kiss as they did so.

'Fancy a fuck before the pub?' said Clive.

'Later,' said Kieran, 'whatever you want.' Though there was every chance that a happy boozy stupor would over-take them on the way to bed and the next they'd know would be waking with bodies improbably entwined half-way through Sunday morning.

Finally they were both ready, regarding each other across the high-ceilinged, book-filled living room.

'Ready?'

'Ready.'

'I do still like your flat,' said Kieran, as they went downstairs. 'By the way, how's...?' He gestured towards the door of the flat below.

'She's fine. Getting dottier, if possible, but very very sweet. She's away on holiday. Brighton, I think.'

'Heavens!'

'Oh, she wouldn't even bat an eyelid if she found herself in *that* side of Brighton. She's entirely non-judgemental. That's not my jargon, by the way.' The owner of the flat was a large middle-aged lady called Cath, heavily addicted to cheap wine and Burmese cats. They had called her Cath the Cat, except that her most recent Burmese had developed a fondness for sleeping in the tumble-dryer, with terminal consequences. Clive wondered whether the Burmese which now roamed Salisbury Road was some kind of poor relation.

He closed the street door behind them and in a fidgety way double-checked both locks.

'Yes, I like the flat,' said Kieran again, 'but it really is in a quite ridiculous place.'

'Well, I wasn't to know. It seemed a good idea at the

time.'

And so it had. Clive had originally bought, on a long and advantageous lease, the top two floors of the house in Salisbury Road: the attic was to be his studio, office, and ultimately the hub of his publishing empire; the floor beneath was to provide his living accommodation. That much of the plan had, in a manner of speaking, worked out. What had not worked out was the locality. Clive had gambled that Salisbury Road would become gentrified, move artily up-market like some other bits of North and East London, and for a while that seemed to be happening. Then - with what seemed like suddenness though it must have taken months - the planners had sliced off half the street with a new dual-carriageway, leaving the stub in which Clive lived; the new road in turn spawned a new shopping centre, and Salisbury Road's grocer's, newsagent's, and quite marvellous ironmonger's all died not particularly lingering deaths. Now the road was a decaying anachronism with alternating fragments of gentility and dereliction, and anyone trying to locate it in an old A-Z had to be gently directed to the end which still actually led somewhere. In the latest edition it was indexed but invisible.

They took the short cut to the pub, through a wide and quite handsome pedestrian alley which some grandiose former local authority had thought fit to dignify with an ornate Inns-of-Courtish gas-lamp. It was well-lit but generally deserted, and they walked through it in an easy, affectionate semi-embrace. Then they emerged onto a disenfranchised main street which must once have thought of itself as a rival for the nearby A10: certainly the pub, The Clarendon, had ambitions of the coaching-inn sort - a Georgian stuccoed front with an absurdly large semi-circular glazed hood fronting an archway which must once have led to stables and which now led to the saloon bar, tucked discreetly back from the street. The Clarendon wasn't a gay pub - you wouldn't find it in the listings - but it was very clearly sympathetic. Clive assumed this to be mostly due to the landlord, a married but subversively

43

theatrical Welshman whom he called Gwylim, after the maniac in some half-remembered Dylan Thomas story, except when he called him Gwyneth instead. Now Gwylim, or Gwyneth, wearing a shirt apparently constructed of yellow and orange tropical vegetation, welcomed them with much the same gleaming smile as the crocodile in *Alice* must have welcomed the little fishes.

'Good evening,' he said sweetly. 'And what can you possibly have done to entice him from the bright lights of Earl's Court? It can't be Mother's Day again. Two pints of our finest?'

Alex, the other barman, rolled his eyes towards the ceiling. He was twentyish, seriously on the way to chubbyness rather than chunkyness, but blue-eyed, blond crew-cut, and fun. It had taken Clive a long while to work out that Alex, who these days addressed him as 'Dear' with a complete lack of either edge or campness, was gay. He liked Alex, whom he didn't at all fancy, for that reassuring, sane complicity across the bar.

'And how are we today?' continued Gwylim, ingratiatingly to Kieran, as he delivered the overflowing glasses. 'Have we been hobnobbing with the famous? Oh, of course, I forgot. You come here to do that, don't you?' And he was gone, to the till, and then to another customer.

'Well,' said Kieran, casting a predatory eye around the bar, 'the gang's all here.'

They were. In retrospect, Clive thought, this might well come to be seen as the Clarendon's summer. Through the long hot evenings of July and on into this moodily warm August, the bar had been steadily filling up with beautiful boys. Some were with girlfriends, of course, and others were formed into those tight threatening little knots of straight machismo, but there was a clear undercurrent of something else. Ginger but winsome Gary, for instance, with a friend who was all bleached hair and gesture; or enigmatic Steve, dark, laughing, as always in jeans and striped rugby shirt, whom Clive had taken home one evening and then, simply and happily, talked with all night over two bottles of wine. He didn't know about Steve really, he remained not at all unpleasantly a teasingly perpetual object of desire. Other objects of desire, less interesting and less easily named, had passed fleetingly through his hands.

If there was an undercurrent, there was also a sediment, and here was Claude, bearded and boozed and sixty, leering over towards them.

'I've just been listening to some of the conversation in this place,' he said, spilling his gin, 'and they're all so bloody serious. *So* bloody serious. I tell you. It makes me sick, all these young people with nothing better to do than sit around on their arses talking about mortgages and cars. Tell you what, I'm looking for someone to upset.'

'You've plenty of choice today, Claude.'

'Too bloody right I have. Who's this?' He squinted approvingly at Kieran. 'Do I know you? If not, why bloody not?' He turned back to Clive. 'Is he with you? Good for you, you lucky old bastard.' And with a nudge so vigorous that it almost sent Clive's beer flying, he wandered away in search of someone to upset.

In his sour way, Claude was right: too many of the half-bright young things - those who had been financial brokers last year and estate agents the year before that - seemed to speak only the hard acquisitive argot of the time. Further down the bar, however, was a more promising group: Tim, a mid-thesis PhD student working on the European historical novel; Geoff, his brother, a radical carpenter; Dylan, an extremely hairy boy who was studying philosophy; and Gavin, the Scotsman with the famous ears. There was no sign yet of Philip from Tesco's.

'Sore feet?' asked Tim.

Clive laughed. 'Not really. It wasn't that strenuous. Anyway, we spent half the time watching the crowd go by. You should have been there.'

'I suppose I should really. After all it was about free speech - what's left of it - more than anything else. So what happened when you all got there? I mean' - he winked at his brother - 'was it all "ideologically sound"?' He formed the quotation marks in the air with a finger and thumb of each hand as he spoke.

'We didn't really stay to find out. There were a *lot* of people and it was very sticky and there was nothing worth drinking.'

'And,' said Kieran, 'there was this utterly disastrous Scottish comedian. Sorry,' he said to the ears, 'that's not a racist remark, but he was *terrible*.'

Kieran, the two brothers, and Gavin seemed about to become enmeshed in a conversation about the march or the state of Scottish comedy, so Clive turned to the philosopher who was so ludicrously though not inappropriately called Dylan.

'Done anything remarkable today then?'

'Not a lot, mate,' said Dylan agreeably, implying something momentous. 'I've been thinking about tomatoes mostly.'

'Yes?'

'It's an essay I was supposed to have handed in last term. About whether a ripe tomato is necessarily red.'

'You mean whether we think of red as necessarily the colour of a ripe tomato, or whether we could learn to think of tomato-colour as something other than red, or....'

'That sort of thing.'

'I think if I'd studied philosophy I'd have gone madder.'

'Probably, mate, probably.'

'There are yellow tomatoes in Tesco's, by the way.'

'That's beside the point.' For a moment Dylan looked quite cross. 'So,' he went on, 'you've been marching n support of freedom today, have you?'

'Yes.'

'That's another dodgy concept. Freedom, free-will. No-one takes it seriously any more.'

'I do.'

'Well yes, you would, mate, because you're just an old hippie really.'

Coming from a boy with practically waist-length hair, this seemed a bit much, but Clive let that pass. 'No it's not. It's just that being a gay agnostic - no ties, no beliefs - I've paradoxically no choice but to believe in freedom. I have to believe that choices are constantly open to me, even when I choose not to avail myself of them. And that sense of freedom confers a special moral responsibility not on a church or a state but on me. It makes me aware that I *could* decide to do something daft - like jump through a plate-glass window or hurt or damage myself in some other way. My freedom must include the essential option to do things which other people might reckon are silly or bad for me.'

'Then why did you give up smoking?' asked Dylan, lighting a cigarette.

'Okay, because it was bad for me. But more importantly because it was a choice over which I had total control and which I chose to exercise.'

'Right, but the number of choices over which you have that kind of control is fairly restricted. I mean, you can decide not to smoke, or you can decide to drink bitter rather than lager, and so on, but even when you get to something as relatively mundane as the plate-glass window it seems highly unlikely that it presents a real choice. You're not actually thinking about jumping through one.'

'Why not?'

'Because if you were,' said Dylan pragmatically, 'you'd be a nutcase.'

'Well, I still see the concept of free-will, of potentiality if you like, as an intellectual raft. I couldn't bear to imagine that we're trapped. I want to envisage a world fit for free people to live in. Who said that? Iris Murdoch?'

'Simone de Beauvoir,' said Kieran, who had suddenly slipped back into the conversation. 'Well, it might as well have been. Actually, dear, you simply want to have your cake and eat it as usual. Your brand of free-will allows you to be as cautious as you like in practice in the safe knowledge that you can be as reckless as you like in theory.'

'Well said.' Dylan was delighted. 'That's worth another pint. Anyone care for one?'

'I'll get them,' said Clive. 'It's time I bought you one.'

'Well, if it helps prove your freedom. It's Guinness. The

bitter's revolting.'

Alex, operating on barman's radar, had appeared from nowhere and had already started off the Guinness.

'And one for yourself,' said Clive.

'Cheers, dear, I'll have a half of something lethal.'

When Clive had paid for the drinks, Dylan said, 'He called you "dear". That's a bit much, mate.'

'He does, he does. He's a poppet.' To his considerable pleasure, Clive caught Kieran looking momentarily a bit concerned.

'Is he taking the piss?' Dylan asked.

'No, he's just another faggot, that's all.'

'Is he heck. I used to go to school with him. He's as straight as I am.'

'You mean he didn't fancy you enough to make a grab in the showers.'

'You're incorrigible,' said Dylan with only half-feigned disgust.

'Encouragable,' said Clive.

The lights flickered lower, apparently portending a power-cut, but it was only Gwylim playing with the dimmers to create 'atmosphere'. Rugby-shirted Steve was pushing his way through the crowded gloom towards them.

'Hello Clive, my old son,' he said. It was a peculiarly irritating greeting, but somehow he got away with it. 'Hello Kieran. How's things?'

Since neither could think of a proper reply to this perennially absurd question, both said 'Fine.'

'And,' Clive added as if by a reflex, 'how about you?'

'Marvellous.' Perpetually smiling Steve positively beamed. 'Off to Europe on Monday. A few days in Paris, then all points south via Interail. I reckon on being away two months.'

'By yourself?'

'No, I'm going with Nick.' He said it without innuendo, and didn't respond to Clive's amused, questioning raised eyebrow. Nick was a famously pretty boy and every bit as sexually enigmatic as Steve.

'Lucky you. What about your job?'

'Resigned. Told them to stuff it, in fact. I've been saving for this for ages.'

'Chucked up everything and just cleared off,' said Kieran.

'Something like that,' said Steve, puzzled.

'Larkin,' Clive explained. 'An improbable mutual hero of ours. It's amazing the way those phrases do keep popping up everywhere - memorable speech indeed. Anyway, I *do* approve. I don't think it's at all a deliberate step backwards when someone actually does it. I just wish I could.'

'But you have,' said Steve. 'I mean, you don't have a job that pays you a regular salary anymore. You've done it already.'

'But I do have a probably unsaleable flat and a mortgage and a great heap of half-finished projects. They all tie me down.'

'I thought,' said Dylan, who had been ruminating over his Guinness, 'that you were the one who believed in free-will.'

'All right, I believe in it even when I can't necessarily enact it. Ethics based solely on what one could actually do at this moment wouldn't be very impressive as ethics.'

'But ethics based on things you can't possibly do are just bloody pointless. Or hypocritical.'

'I've never,' said Kieran happily, 'thought a great deal of ethics.'

'Pighead,' Clive replied. 'No, that's not the start of another animal game.' As he turned, smiling, to Kieran, he noticed something that a mutual friend had recently pointed out to him: Kieran, in a crowd like this one, actually became possessive of him in a probably unconscious and wholly reassuring way. He had moved close enough for Clive to put an arm round his shoulders: that was about the limit at the Clarendon, and kissing was very definitely out unless at or after a thoroughly drunken closing-time. Sod it, thought Clive, and gave Kieran a swift kiss. Kieran, meanwhile, was registering the influx of

49

a new young crowd which included the ubiquitous Philip, for once without his leather jacket, dressed in a plain black t-shirt and jeans.

'He may be straight,' said Kieran in his tactless whisper, 'but he's certainly one for the wank bank.' He had a considerable stock of these rhyming obscenities.

'Wouldn't mind getting your gums round his plums?' Clive countered.

'Indeed not. Hang on, dear, one of us is in luck. He's coming this way.'

But Philip, winsomely tossing his immaculate long blond hair, only crossed the bar to acknowledge their presence and to ask without much interest how the march had gone before rejoining his other friends. 'See you later,' he said.

THREE

Things were. There are days and places where the past is omnipresent. Jeremy has walked south along the coast, beyond the jollifications of the yacht club, beyond the fortifications of the Martello tower, along the narrow path on the river-bank and above the narrow shingle strip which separates the river from the sea. Things were. He knows that Slaughden, where the yacht club is now, was once a port with a customs house: Crabbe's father was saltmaster there. He knows that in the present century it was a populated part of the town, with its own pub, the Three Mariners, demolished by the combined forces of sea and river. And here, what was here? Probably not much, for once, before erosion created this long spur of shingle, Sudbourne Beach, the river-mouth must have been around here. Things were. Now even the track along the river-bank is overgrown with weeds of such surprising luxuriance that Ben, having had his swim, has opted for the treadmill of shingle, leaving Jeremy in solitary conflict with the foliage.

Jeremy has been dreaming a lot recently, and some of the dreams are stacking up into a sequence. They began intermittently, years ago, and they are all set in a town which he is sure doesn't exist but which he has come to know intimately. It has, for instance, two parallel streets, one of which ends in a long shady bend around a raised, walled churchyard, and between the streets there are a number of inns with courtyards behind them, so that it's possible pleasantly to weave in and out of them alternately through front bars and yards. At one point the main street widens into an irregular three-sided market-place with a particularly grand gabled house in one corner. The streets and inns have names, but once awake he can never remember them. What he can remember is that one night he somehow strayed in his dream townscape from the

51

streets he was beginning to know so well and found himself in other streets he knew even better - those of the town in which he now lives. The town he has invented, or re-invented, in his dreams is under the sea.

Last night in his dream he was walking along a raised promenade by a river when suddenly he turned to notice a flight of steps down towards densely-grouped buildings. He walked towards them, passing on his right a large timbered hotel, then turned into an alley alongside it, where there was an open-doored bar with a sign saying 'Smoke Room', and at the end of the alley found himself once again in the main street of the original town. He retraced his steps and only then, near waking, did it occur to him actually within the dream that the roads were unusually narrow and overhung with projecting storeys. The moment of surprise at something which his dream-self would have taken for granted jolted him into wakefulness, and he never returned to the river.

Fully awake, he began to rework and to develop his theories about the dream-town - though he knows that his conscious speculations are subject to various manipulative temptations, such as rationalisation or fictive plotting or simple wishful thinking. He is certain, at least, that the dreams substantially take place before an earlier storm, probably that of 1779. But in that case the engraved glass door of the bar with 'Smoke Room' on it is wrong, for he has already, this morning, with toast and marmalade and magnifying glass checked with the *OED* and found the first citation of 'Smoke Room' dated 1883. But - again - if this pioneering, precocious 'Smoke Room' had been under the sea for over a century by then, even the *OED* wouldn't have stood a chance of hearing about it. Jeremy enjoys these speculative quandaries, though they don't get him anywhere.

Much more worrying, more emotionally perplexing, is the question of what he should do about it all. If it is, say, 1778, in the dream-town, shouldn't he stir the sailors and fishermen from their briar-pipes and their ale, and urge them to move inland before their homes and livelihoods are destroyed? That of course is pure science-fiction, the kind of thing that John Wyndham would have called a chronoclasm. It is, moreover, a type of action which the dream-world wouldn't accommodate, and if by some mistake it did, the result would be simple and instantaneous: he would wake up. Yet, suppose that the past is signalling to the present rather than the present to the past: do the dreams indicate the imminence of another great storm and, if so, shouldn't Jeremy be warning the locals even now to move to higher ground?

He ponders all this with the indulgent self-absorption of the practised sea-gazer. And today, indeed, the sea is disarmingly benign. The onshore breeze has lost its northerly bite, the sky is dotted with the merest fluff of white cloud, and out on the horizon a Harwich-bound liner is glinting in the sunlight like a freshly-unpacked toy. This quite convincing attempt at summer has enticed Jeremy to discard his habitual sweater, and as he stands on the river-bank in jeans and sleeveless shirt the mere impact of sea-breeze and sunlight on his bare arms seems, again, to displace him from the here-and-now. Such intimate, innocent contact between flesh and the elements recalls childhood summers in the long back gardens of the North Kent suburb where he grew up: a world apparently limitless though bounded, as it happens, by brambles, nettles, and the embankment carrying the railway line to Charing Cross. For a moment, he recaptures the sense of all the world existing in a single space.

It is, however, only for a moment. Out at sea, the toy ship has inched away, and a couple of fishing-boats have materialised from nowhere. Jeremy turns back towards the town, discovering as he does so that there is after all still some northerly sharpness in the breeze. Nearing the Martello tower, he crosses from river-bank to sea-wall, soon descending to the more sheltered air on the other side, where the shingle beach meets the giant stepped concrete slabs at the base of the wall. There is a breakwater here which has to be revisited, touched like a charm: it is the one, masked by the Martello tower from the yacht club and the town, from which he once decided he would walk into the sea to his death.   That period of despair, quite genuine and completely out of control as it was, passed, so that now the breakwater is a symbol of survival and continuity.   He sits on it, midway down the beach and facing the sea, hugging his knees up to his chest before reaching around for some stones large enough to lob at the water.   The first throw is unnoticed by Ben, who only looks up with mild interest when he hears the splash.   The second, however, is unignorable, so with an air of dutiful folly the dog lollops into the water, coming to a sudden four-square halt where he judges that the stone might have fallen and assuming an air of aggrieved puzzlement on discovering that it isn't floating in front of him. Accordingly, he plunges his head into the water, emerging with a lump of driftwood which bears no resemblance whatever to a stone but which apparently satisfies him sufficiently for him to deliver it to Jeremy who has by now reclined full-length on the breakwater.   This done, Ben shakes himself vigorously, spraying both breakwater and Jeremy with a doggy dew.

'Okay.'   Jeremy stands up.   'Come on then, Herbert. Dog-brain.'

Once past the yacht club, man and dog cut back to the river-bank which here, where Slaughden once stood, turns inland, past the long-burnt-out wreck of a houseboat, towards Snape.   This too is part of the ritual, especially on summer weekends when the town begins to fill up with day-trippers towards midday, fractious families looking for non-existent sand and elderly couples inexplicably asleep in parked cars.   Here, where the river bends, things were. Ordnance Survey maps of only thirty years ago mark a ferry from the deserted meadowland on the other side of the river, and the nearest sizeable buildings are still called Ferry Farm.   Half a mile or so further upstream, a ragged narrow lane straggles towards the river and peters out in a maze of farm-tracks. It is called High Street, and it must once have been part of the next river-port, Iken. Such things matter to Jeremy, for whom the present consists of successively overlaid pasts, as if a canvas had been used and re-used in such a way that the contours of earlier paintings dimly but insistently suggest themselves. People who know him slightly are inclined to feel that this represents some sort of introspective, self-indulgent opting-out from contemporary reality. Closer friends suspect that Jeremy's way of looking is more difficult and uncomfortable than that.

For a way of looking is what it is, like Wordsworth's urge to 'see into the life of things'. It is impossible, now, as the river follows its long and apparently pointless loop around meadows, not to wonder what this placid and perverse waterway is up to. What it *was* up to, when it abandoned the obvious course of emptying itself into the sea at Slaughden and set out instead on the thankless journey which would end at Orford Ness. What it must have been like for the citizens of Suffolk, reasonably assuming the river to be as sensible and set in its ways as they were, as the unthinkable began to happen before their eyes, here as at Dunwich earlier. And what, Jeremy wonders, was here, exactly here, when Crabbe's father sat in his custom-house collecting the salt-tax? Or when, two hundred years before that, Tudor craftsmen were busily building in their town centre the moot hall which now stands on the seafront?

Someone is walking towards him along the track on the river-bank, and since the track is about six inches wide there is no possibility of avoiding a meeting, unless one of them jumps idiotically into the long and quite possibly boggy grass. It is in any case someone he knows. Oddly, once he gets even a few hundred yards inland, it is almost always someone he knows. It is as if visitors sense that they are somehow under an obligation to stare at the sea and that the subtler pleasures of the river-walk are out of bounds to them. It is the boy who left the pub just before him on Friday evening, and who is neither a surfer nor a fisherman but a musician. Or he was a musician and is now a globe-trotter who every so often comes back to base to work restlessly for six months with computers in

Ipswich before setting off again. He is called Steve, and he has eyes the colour of freshly-opened horse-chestnuts, and he is wearing the brightest green t-shirt Jeremy has ever seen, an offence somehow compounded by the fact that Jeremy's own shirt is a brilliant golden orange.

They meet. They clash. 'Sun,' says Steve, simply.

'Wonderful,' says Jeremy. 'Wrong colour to show off a suntan, though.'

'Parrot colours for summer,' says Steve, laughing. 'See you.'

They sidle past each other, grinningly executing a little hands-on-shoulders dance as they do so. And soon, when Jeremy next turns to look, Steve is a disconcertingly remote green shape far away down the river towards the sea.

Some way ahead, and not at all green, are other disconcerting shapes. Silos. Industrial farming. They are, it's true, nowhere near as offensive as that obtuse and poisonous fortress of a power station which squats on the shore a few miles up the coast. But they are too insistently and simplistically of the present for Jeremy, who now turns away from the river, on a path across the fields with little bridges over big ditches. Ben has gone on ahead, as if programmed for home, turning only occasionally with a cursory glance over his shoulder to make sure Jeremy hasn't forgotten the way. Quite soon, however, he is halted by a gate which will have to be opened for him and - if there's anyone about, which there is - he has also to endure the ridiculous performance of having a lead snapped on to his collar. Ben, being merely a dog, doesn't actually think this is daft, but the attitude he adopts leaves no doubt about what he would think if he could.

Allotments. Jeremy likes the allotments. He likes the crazy gestures of containment, the arbitrary degrees of neglect and care, the occasional grand attempt at comprehensiveness in a tiny space. If landscape is an epic poem, an allotment is an epigram. It has to have its wits about it: it has, if possible, to achieve a pithy epigrammatic juxtaposition of flowers and vegetables. Clematis and runner beans, sharing in their different seasons the same

56

nautical-looking construction of sticks and timbers (but then, he remembers, weren't runner beans originally grown for their flowers and only eaten as it were accidentally?). Allotted space. Allotted time. With their pleasing combination of congruence and chance, allotments seem to be a good image. Of something.

Of the world made manageable, certainly, but also of the world distilled: a quintessence.

He walks towards the town, passing tall trees with rookeries, tennis courts in desultory Sunday morning use: he knows the players by sight, and exchanges nods with them. Ben, now unleashed again, trots along the footpath, sniffing the air. They wander along a shady unmade road, into Park Lane, and soon find themselves at the top of the Town Steps. Jeremy stops, looking across the happily random townscape at the sea beyond. 'Look, Ben,' he says, and the dog obligingly plants his forepaws on the wall in order to peer over it and bark at a surprised passing gull.

It was perhaps at this point that Jeremy, all those years ago, decided that eventually - after suburbia, after London - this would be his place. It was the summer vacation of 1967, the summer of 'A Whiter Shade of Pale', and he'd never been to East Anglia before. What happened seemed to have been an epiphany - he'd been reading Joyce, and the word had stuck - in which the disparate co-ordinates of time and place had suddenly and mysteriously locked into their proper, perfect relationship. Somehow, he'd known, he'd end up here, and not just because of the gulls and the curlews, the collisions of nature and art, the ghosts of Crabbe and Britten - he hadn't foreseen all the associations, had never heard of Crabbe and hardly listened to Britten, he simply knew that the place had *duende*. And it was a place at the end of a road, at the edge of an island, on a thoroughfare to nowhere. To be here at all was an act of particularly deliberate choice.

Jeremy doesn't know - for even the short history of his memory is silted up to that extent - whether he felt all these things as he stood at the top of the Town Steps in 1967. Nor does he know for sure about another moment which

57

must have come quite soon after; the moment somewhere in the late sixties when we threw the world away. Not a single moment, of course: a whole kaleidoscope of separate events shaken into a wholly unexpected pattern of destruction. Just when so much seemed to have been affirmed, so much love and generosity taken on board. Yes, it had been a good time, Procul Harum's summer: Jeremy had met his first real lover, smoked his first real dope, and discovered his destiny.

Strangely, and worryingly, it doesn't seem so long ago.

FOUR

'Not much chance of play.'

'I'm sorry.'

'In the Test. I thought you followed cricket.'

'I do when I can. I've been following other things lately.'

'Yes of course.' Detective Inspector Bob Clarke looked momentarily puzzled, as if the idea of putting work - even work for him - before cricket were mildly blasphemous. 'And what's the story so far?'

'Nothing definite. One or two leads from Saturday.'

'I'll need something on paper before the end of the week.'

'No problem.' Why, Andy wondered, was he sitting here saying *No problem*? Why wasn't he saying *What the hell for*? 'Though to be honest, sir, it all seems a bit dodgy, even for us.'

'I'll decide that. Give me some edited highlights.'

'Well, there's certainly something to be pinned on Baxter, but I'm also interested in this editor bloke Greenslade. Even though I don't think he's got anything to tell us, I'd like to frighten him a bit just to see where he jumps. I know he's probably got some influential friends, and legally he seems as pure as the driven, but....'

'In that case, leave the influential friends and, come to that, leave Greenslade for a bit longer if you can bear to. He may have the means to make a fuss if you do something daft. Start with his *un*influential friends. Find someone to put the pressure on without getting questions asked in the House. At least, not the wrong questions, and not yet.'

'I should be able to manage that. Greenslade was on the march on Saturday with a young friend who also seems to have had some earlier connection with the honourable member himself. If you see what I mean. Now he could be a lemon worth squeezing.'

59

Bob Clarke stared vacantly out at the drizzle and played with a paper-clip which he was apparently trying to bend into the shape of a cricket-bat. The man's obsessed, thought Andy.

'Squeeze him then. But do try not to break any bones. He isn't a bloody terrorist. And remember, what we want is evidence on Baxter - no side-effects, no flak, and absolutely nothing in the press until I say so. Get some evidence, and fast, and make it good, and after that you can start bringing in the celebrities.'

'You mean, just to get their autographs?' Andy grinned sheepishly.

'Yes, on the ends of nice juicy statements. Meanwhile, what do you know about this rent boy?'

'Oh, I wouldn't say he's really a rent boy,' said Andy, suddenly feeling almost protective of Kieran.

'He will be when the Sunday papers get the story. And that's another thing: we could do with some photographs along with the statement. Use your initiative. Anyway, what do you know about him?'

'Not a lot, but I'm checking this morning.'

'We've got a file on him?'

'Oh yes. He's quite a lad in those circles.'

'Then pick him up. On second thoughts, I probably do mean pick him up. You know where to find him?'

'It shouldn't be difficult.'

'Then haul him in. We want names and addresses of all relevant contacts. A photograph which looks the part. And something simple and signed which is strong enough to drop Baxter in it. I've already had the *Sunday Herald* on the phone this morning. They know in their bones we should have a leak for them. Any permutation of "rent boy", "teenage" and "Aids" will do, as long as Martin Baxter's name's firmly attached to it. Quite apart from which, him indoors is getting impatient.'

'You mean, he's actually pressing us on this?'

'No, Andrew, it's a figure of speech. But the vibes I'm getting from around Whitehall suggest that they'd like some action. They want Baxter knocked off his pedestal, of course, for obvious political reasons, but there's a bit more to it than that. They'll look pretty bloody silly if they've put about all this subversive gay conspiracy stuff and then they find there isn't one.'

'And is there?'

Bob Clarke swivelled towards the window for a moment and with the end of his striped tie flicked something, a speck of scepticism perhaps, from his left cuff. Then he turned back to Andy.

'It depends on what you mean. If I were a rational private citizen, I'd probably have to say no, it's a load of baloney. But I'm not. I'm a public servant, and that means that in some rather tortuous way I'm instructed by and responsible to the public. And because we live in what we're pleased to call a democracy, it's our job to enact the will of the people as conveyed through their elected government. The government perceives a conspiracy - though that may be a posh way of saying that it sees a way to destabilise the opposition - and the press perceives a conspiracy. It's our job to find it if it exists, though I just hope it's not our job to invent it if it doesn't. I think I might find that distasteful.' He looked hard at Andy. 'But we're not moralists, remember. Leave that to judges and vicars.'

'Right.' Andy smiled privately.

'I suppose it *must* be raining at the Oval.' Bob Clarke flicked on the portable radio on his desk. The sound of a soprano singing something in German filled the room, and both men stared at the radio in incredulous dismay before the Inspector flicked it off again. 'Thought so. Now go and play with your files. The phone's about to ring.'

As Andy closed the door behind him, it did. He walked along a corridor which seemed almost pathologically unsure of its own identity. When the building had been a grocery warehouse, this must have been the accounts department: the office doors had fancy mouldings and complicated obscure glass panels which suggested a fruitless attempt to gentrify the business of invoices and statements. Now, overlaid on that, were traces of the utilitarian male dinginess to be found in any run-down nick: notices and posters pinned artlessly on the walls, stained teacups parked on ledges, reverberant echoes from under-furnished rooms. There was the clinging residual smell of old disinfectant and older dirt. He took the stairs rather than the lift, the brass handrail gleaming only from the constant polishing of use.

Back in his basement office, Andy turned his attention to the VDU. 'RX2498315C RADFORD KIERAN JAMES DOB 250567,' it said, 'KNOWN CONTACTS.' There followed a bizarre list of the once-famous, the almost-famous, and the wholly unknown. The other details were on the whole disappointingly apolitical and unsubversive - Kieran, it seemed, was mostly interested in having a good time - but some points puzzled Andy. What, for instance, did 'MEM NPS' mean? He could presumably find out; meanwhile, he had to regret the data compiler's mania for unexplained abbreviation. The medical details, he noted with mild distaste, included rather too many out-patient visits to a particular London hospital but nothing more instructive. Fucking doctors and their precious confidentiality, he thought, and then: better be a bit careful with him, just in case - we don't want blood. All he could really learn about Kieran's health involved childish ailments like chicken pox and later persistent trouble with a wisdom tooth. At the end of the entry Andy added the information he had noted on the pad in front of him: 'MOST RECENT KNOWN CONTACTS: PHILPOTTS RALPH BERTRAM FLAT 1 24 SWINBURNE GARDENS SW 10: GREENSLADE CLIVE ANDREW 35B SALISBURY ROAD N 17.'

'We're not moralists,' Bob Clarke had said. Well, that was certainly true enough, but were judges and vicars really any different? Bent judge stories were as easy to come up with as bent MP stories, to say nothing of bent coppers, and as for the clergy.... He remembered the infuriating, infallible common-sense of his father's sermons which, in their studied demotic artlessness, had the same simple consistency as prime ministerial speeches. His father was an admirable vicar, no doubt about that: efficient, energetic, up-to-date, committed to high-profile good causes, modern liturgy, and discos in the church hall. Of course, all that didn't stop him being a self-serving careerist, with his eye on a bishopric, who wore fancy dress and spoke in a silly voice on Sundays.

Fuck the morality, thought Andy, let's get on with the action.

Bob Clarke had said that he wasn't to touch Greenslade yet, but he had his own reasons - that article in *Pendulum* for one - for indulging in a little arm's length frightening. His mates in the New Britain Campaign could see to that: they owed him a favour, and it seemed no more than natural justice that the favour should involve settling up with Greenslade. He'd got them off a charge of mugging outside Heaven when he was on his first gay surveillance job a few months back - even though he'd been there, even though he'd seen Wayne put the boot in so far it gave new meaning to the phrase - through a lack of positive identification. The light was bad, there was no proof, he couldn't be sure. The magistrate had been as sarcastic as he dared about Andy's powers of eyesight and memory, but that was all - except that the story, with a strong suggestion of police connivance in the attack, and names withheld only for legal reasons, had turned up in Greenslade's mag. Wayne had sent the victim, who was then recovering in hospital, a bunch of pink roses with a card from 'Your mates in Villiers Street': you had to admit he had a sense of humour. Andy dialled Wayne's number and asked for his extension.

'Hello, Wayne? It's Andy.'

'Hello, you old crook. It's good to hear from you. You must want something.'

'Only if you've nothing better to do.'

'For you, anything.' Wayne chuckled.

'Is it okay to talk?'

Wayne hesitated. 'Best be on the safe side. I'll call you back on a direct line.' A few moments later Andy's phone rang. 'Hello again. Tell me more.'

'You remember that bent writer who tried to stitch me up in some poxy little magazine?'

63

'Yeah, sure.'

'Okay, can I give you an address? It's Clive Greenslade, 35b Salisbury Road, N 17. Got that?'

'Anything else?'

'Drinks in a local pub called the Clarendon. Not a poofter's pub as such - "mixed" is the word, I think.'

'And that's it?'

'That's it. Nothing drastic, just a warning. Make him know how much we care about him. If I can, I'll get down there myself, discreetly of course, so you can pass a little extra message on for me. It all helps.'

'Fine. Sounds like a good night out for a weekday. How's Debbie?'

'Okay, apart from she's down in fucking Southampton on some bloody vocational course or other.'

'I never could understand what she sees in a shit like you.'

'Neither can I. Cheers, Wayne.'

He put the phone down. The likes of Wayne would inherit the earth. Now, for instance, he'd be sitting in his plush office and his immaculate suit, shovelling around huge sums of invisible money for a leading city institution; later, transformed in DMs and jeans and Union Jack t-shirt, he'd happily lay into any pinko poof with just the same gutsy relish. Wayne was a creature, if not a caricature, of the times: a truly prosperous yob. Andy admired that. Indulging his sense of humour, Wayne had recently bought himself a Mark II Jaguar, like the one Inspector Morse used to have: the odd thing was that it perfectly complemented both his selves. Andy was glad he hadn't been tempted to mention Philpotts to Wayne: age bestowed some small measure of sanctity, even in his eyes, and that was a visit he'd have to make himself, later in the week, after he'd sorted young Kieran out tomorrow evening. Meanwhile, he'd some real routine paperwork to get on with, and this evening he quite fancied an undercover pint in N 17: perhaps he should take Greg along to broaden his education, but perhaps not.

Andy stretched idly in his chair, then stood up. He felt

restless, unused: it was always like that when he hadn't seen Debbie for a while. Picking up his briefcase, and taking the top sheet of paper from the pad on his desk, he crossed his office and entered an ante-room - a cramped recess with a second door leading out of it and crammed with old shadowy bits of office furniture including an ancient filing cabinet. Andy opened the second drawer down and dropped the sheet from his pad with the two addresses into the Radford file: he didn't believe in entrusting things entirely to the memory of a computer. Then he took a key from his pocket and opened the locked top drawer, which didn't contain files on anyone. Almost furtively he removed from his briefcase a pair of handcuffs and added them to the contents of the drawer - rubber gloves, straps, truncheons, black box with a tangle of wires. For a moment he stood there in totally rapt absorption, like a child lost in contemplation of his favourite toys.

* * *

By the time they reached their seats in the theatre, Bertram had been greeted by at least six people and had managed to recognise two of them. He slumped heavily into his seat, exhausted partly by the affability his presence seemed to engender and partly by his clothes. He was wearing, as always on such occasions, a very old and very heavy blue-grey suit, a white shirt far too tight around the neck, and a monstrously patterned silk tie. The handkerchief in his jacket breast pocket, folded and placed with a precision which would have taken anyone else half the afternoon, was for him a habit which happened without looking or thinking. Habit had nevertheless overdressed him for this sultry evening, and Kieran was glad of the toy-boyish liberty which allowed him to wear nothing but a salmon-pink shirt and thin pair of lemon-coloured cotton trousers. 'Very fetching, my dear,' Bertram had said when they met. 'I suppose you're the brown bread.' Now he looked about him anxiously.

65

'Well, my dear, I do hope there's no-one else who thinks they know me around here. After all, I might want to say something rude.' He paused. 'Or fart,' he added as an afterthought.

'Who are they all, anyway?'

'Failed authors, I expect. Prostrating themselves before a walking rejection-slip.'

'Still, it's odd of them to remember you.' Kieran laughed, and put his hand on Bertram's knee. 'Oh, that sounds awful. I don't mean it like that. I mean, if they're all failed authors, they must have met a lot of rejection-slips in their time.'

'Ah yes, but only one from Whiting & Hammond. They probably think of me as the great chance they missed.' Bertram guffawed suddenly. 'Well really, I expect they're just men I fucked and forgot. You know the sort.'

Kieran wasn't to be drawn. 'I'm not sure I'm quite old enough to have forgotten.'

'Oh no? I thought you had more in common with Cressida than that.'

'I don't know the play, yet.'

'No, of course. I know it probably better than anything else in Shakespeare, which is odd really, as it used to be so seldom performed. It's very strange to find it in the West End, but I suppose that's one thing we ought to be grudgingly thankful for, all this sponsored Shakespeare everywhere. Though I do sometimes wonder whether the sponsors have the remotest idea of what they're funding. Here for instance we seem to have an insurance company promoting a piece about infidelity, murder, homosexuality and the pox - they certainly wouldn't consider most of the characters for a life policy. And wasn't there once a Japanese car called a Cressida? You know that according to Henryson she died a leper? I can't see how anyone would knowingly wish that even on a tin box on wheels. But I'm rambling.'

'No you're not, dear. It's fascinating. But look, I've got a rough idea of the background and plot, so tell me quickly the three other things that an ignorant boy should know about *Troilus and Cressida* before it begins.'

'Only three? Well, the first is that it's absolutely the most intelligent thing Shakespeare wrote, and that does have the odd drawback. You mustn't for instance let Ulysses bore you to sleep in the second scene with his great speeches about the nature of the universe: they're the dullest things in the play, and they come quite early, and with any luck he'll be strikingly pretty. Though probably, being Ulysses, more striking than pretty. But there is *so* much intelligence: irony, self-parody, wicked juxtapositions of tone and content, breathtaking abrasiveness. Dear me, I sound just like a bloody critic.

'Anyway, that had better count as *one* thing. The second is that the first half seems to be a comedy, the second half seems to be a tragedy, and the whole thing seems to be a chronicle. So it's every kind of renaissance play done up in one bundle. Genre-bending, if you see what I mean.

'And thirdly....' But the house-lights were beginning to fade. 'Oh well, you'll see,' muttered Bertram a little crossly, and elaborately adjusted himself in his seat.

The stage was draped with a great many gauzy translucent shapes which Kieran supposed might come in a later scene to represent tents on the battlefield. What happened now, however, was quite different. Through the gauzes, and until now unperceived because unlit, a baroque architecture of towers and ramparts began to shimmer in the misty amber light of an autumn evening. Then, quite unexpectedly, the extremely ugly hippie at the end of their row leapt into the aisle and pointed at the stage.

'In Troy, there lies the scene,' he said, and began walking towards it. He sneered and snarled his way through the prologue before retreating to a stool placed just to the left of the stage.

'Thersites as prologue and chorus, I should suppose,' said Bertram. 'Not a bad idea. The young William Brannigan would have made a very good Thersites, I've always thought. Here we go.'

A very odd couple had appeared from the wings downstage right. One was a choking old man in a long spattered raincoat. The other was a blond boy in white trousers and vest who was in the process of unbuttoning and flinging aside the merest token of military costume - a sort of red-and-gold jerkin. He was evidently upset about something, and Kieran was surprised to hear him announce himself not merely as a broken-hearted Trojan soldier but as Troilus.

'But I am weaker than a woman's tear,' he said,
'Tamer than sleep, fonder than ignorance,
Less valiant than the virgin in the night,
And skilless as unpractis'd infancy.'

The old man, who had more than a little of the Frankie Howerd camp about him, was not to be impressed. He seemed intent on working Troilus up to an even greater degree of frustrated desire for his niece Cressida before leaving him, with a queenly flourish, to a soliloquy. Then there was Cressida herself, in lilac and jewels, as the gauzes parted leaving her and her servant free access to the now-glowing towers and ramparts. Something worth seeing was about to take place, and soon they were joined by the old man Pandarus who appeared even more eager than his niece to view the Trojan soldiers as they passed by. All of them had their attractions, especially Troilus - despite Cressida's sarcastic comments about him. Finally, she was alone, and she delivered herself of a little soliloquy which was as unexpectedly eloquent as Troilus's corresponding one in the previous scene had been halting. The uncle had shuffled away with an apologetic, syphilitic cough.

'Rum lot, these Trojans,' whispered Kieran.

'My dear, wait until you see the Greeks. The *alternative* Greeks, that is. They come a little later on. Though this lot will do for a start. I bet the gorgeous one turns out to be Diomedes.'

The gauzes had indeed formed themselves into tents, and in front of them the Greeks, dressed in khaki and green camouflage gear, were arranging themselves in a loose circle of canvas chairs; to one side, near Thersites' perch, another pair of Greeks, wearing large straw sunhats, lolled in deck-chairs with their backs to everyone else. If the Trojans were rather determinedly urban, these Greeks were decidedly nomadic, outdoors types. One of them was certainly gorgeous, but he was saying nothing, merely striking a series of disgruntled attitudes while one elder statesman, and then another, spoke at length. Ulysses, as it turned out, was neither striking nor pretty, but a peevish little politician who went on interminably about the nature of order: 'The Idea of Order at Troy West,' muttered Bertram, pleased with himself. In the next scene, the focus shifted to the pair in sunhats, to the horrid hippie Thersites, and to a lumbering oaf called Ajax. Here at last the language seemed to take on a bizarre self-relishing vigour quite distinct from the impassioned but correct diplomatic exchanges which had gone before.

Then there were a lot of truculent Trojans and a mad screaming queen; all the Greeks conspiring to mislead poor thick Ajax; and Pandarus camping it up with a sluttish creature who turned out to be Helen of Troy. During much of this Kieran allowed his attention to drift towards a darkly attractive profile a little way to his right. He knew that there was no point in trying to take in a Shakespeare play properly at one go. It was like listening to a symphony: at first hearing you could get some sense of the shape and mood of the thing, pick out a few interesting details, make mental notes for future reference; but finding out how the piece actually worked would have to wait until later. Now on stage the two lovers seemed to be moving towards a resolution: this must be the 'comedy' false ending of which Bertram had spoken. And it was undeniably intelligent stuff too. 'This is the monstruosity in love, lady,' Troilus was saying, 'that the will is infinite and the execution confined; that the desire is boundless, and the act a slave to limit.' Then Pandarus reappeared, meddlesome as ever, promising to show them to a chamber with bed, before the house lights came up for the interval.

Bertram looked at once smug and irritable, as if he had been storing up some textual quibble from three and a half scenes ago. The dark handsome profile, getting up and making for the bar, turned out to have a complexion like blackcurrant yoghurt. Kieran turned quickly back to Bertram. 'Drink?' he asked hopefully.

'As long as you wriggle your way to the bar to get them,' said Bertram.

The bar was inevitably crammed with people inexpert at the art of managing their drinks in public. Bertram had already been accosted by another half-remembered literary acquaintance when Kieran struggled back to him with their drinks: he was the author of a book about the fifties who, after giving Kieran a sharply disbelieving look, vanished into the crowd. Bertram attacked his glass of overpriced plonk as if he thought himself in imminent danger of dehydration.

'The fifties!' he exclaimed. 'The man wasn't old enough to read and write in the fifties. I do in fact remember him interviewing me for his book. I didn't tell him anything at *all* interesting of course. It's odd to have become a piece of oral history, all the same.' He paused. 'I know what you're thinking. Stop it.'

Kieran laughed. 'It never crossed my mind.'

'Do you like it?'

'What?'

'The play so far.'

'Yes, I think so, though it is complicated. I'm not sure I'm getting all the intricacies. There are an awful lot of words.'

'It *is* wordy,' said Bertram. 'Have you ever noticed that once you get a particular idea in your head, everything you see or read seems to be about it?'

'Yes. Such as?'

'I was thinking about remembering and forgetting - or, more precisely, about being remembered and forgotten. I hadn't noticed before quite how much *Troilus and Cressida* is about that. There's Menelaus, who's hardly given the prominence his status deserves, and old Nestor, whom everyone treats as a joke. Priam's shunted aside by all those sons of his. Achilles, as you'll see in a moment,

70

thinks his fame and honour have been wiped out just because he's done his bit and wants to cuddle up with Patroclus for a while - which strikes me as a perfectly tenable position. So many of the characters are in different ways undervalued, half-forgotten. Like writers. Do you know who I would really have liked to publish?'

'Eliot? Auden? I can't guess.'

'No - though of course if they'd all trooped round to me from Russell Square I wouldn't have slammed the door on them. No, it's the half-forgotten who appeal to me, the writers who for ages seemed to go unaccountably out of print. Joy Scovell. Burns Singer. Phoebe Hesketh. John Heath-Stubbs.'

'William Brannigan.'

'Well yes, and of course I *did* publish him, but he rather wished obscurity upon himself. And that's rather a different thing.' A noteless bell buzzed like a loud wasp. 'Why can't theatres have decent intervals?' Bertram grumbled as he somehow insinuated his empty glass onto a ledge. 'Let's get back before all these other legs put themselves in our way.'

The second half began, as Bertram had said, with Achilles being subjected to a pompous lecture about honour from Ulysses. Then Cressida was taken off to the Greeks in exchange for Antenor - to the dismay of Troilus and to the delight of Diomedes, the gorgeous Greek, who evidently couldn't wait to get his hands on her. Ajax and Hector fought a ridiculous little duel which ended in the discovery that they were cousins, after which everyone on stage seemed to be obscurely related to everyone else and they all got drunk. It was beginning to seem to Kieran a rather lengthy play.

'Now this,' whispered Bertram, 'is a most remarkable scene.' The lights had dimmed to a furtive orange-ochre, and there was a prolonged warble of semi-electronic music which was presumably meant to signal emotional significance. Downstage, partially undressed Cressida and near-naked Diomedes, looking like something out of a Colt calendar, were meeting, observed in the upstage amber

71

shadows by Troilus and Ulysses, while Thersites looked on from his offstage perch. It was almost contrapuntal, this weird interlocking of three separate points of perception: as the scene developed, and as Troilus' appalled anguish became almost unbearable, Kieran began to suspect why, apart from its ingenuity, Bertram had drawn his attention to it. For now the drama onstage began to engage with his own obsession, with his perilous sense of shifting realities, with being and not being. Troilus simply couldn't believe in the existence of the transformed or the alternative Cressida presented before his eyes and, in what seemed a notable burst of early existentialism, he tried to assimilate the idea that there might be more than one Cressida:

'This she? No, this is Diomed's Cressida.
If beauty have a soul, this is not she;
If souls guide vows, if vows be sanctimonies,
If sanctimony be the gods' delight,
If there be rule in unity itself,
This is not she. O madness of discourse,
That cause sets up with and against itself!
Bifold authority! where reason can revolt
Without perdition, and loss assume all reason
Without revolt. This is, and is not, Cressid.'

Kieran tried to snatch a sideways glance at Bertram, but the artful old bugger was peering at the stage in his most inscrutable sphinx-like manner. 'If beauty have a soul....' Bertram, the other evening, had tried to talk him into that, but it was clear that for Troilus this had become a negative proposition, unarguably denied by the reality before him. And what, now, had Bertram really meant before the play when he'd said that Kieran had something in common with Cressida? Simply that he was promiscuous? They both knew that already. Or that Bertram knew - and, what was almost more devastating, Shakespeare had known - the precise ways in which, just as Troilus's Cressida was different from Diomedes' Cressida, so Bertram's Kieran would be different from Clive's Kieran and both were different from the Kieran who'd get picked up in the Pit. All of which was fairly obvious, but it was alarming to see it mirrored before him in such a knowing way. He'd always claimed never to weep, yet now he felt the unfamiliar, surprisingly acidic moisture seeping into his eyes. With relief, he recognised the cause as nothing more serious than transitory self-pity.

Shakespeare followed his big scene with a lot of little scenes and much Act Five-ish military confusion. Yet he still had a surprise or two up his sleeve. Kieran knew that *Troilus and Cressida* must end with the death of Hector and the mourning of Troilus, but he hadn't expected Hector to be hacked about by a gang of leather-jacketed thugs under the enthusiastic direction of Achilles, nor had he anticipated the further characteristic wrench between tone and context which marked Achilles' closing speeches:

'Look, Hector, how the sun begins to set,
How ugly night comes breathing at his heels;
Even with the vail and dark'ning of the sun
To close the day up, Hector's life is done.'

So there it was, the great lost world of heroism and nobility hammered into the ground by thuggish vulgarity, yet accompanied as ever by the mirage of eloquence. It was a bit like London, really.

When Pandarus had shuffled off after the epilogue, and the applause had subsided, and the house lights had come up, Kieran looked at Bertram expecting signs of triumph. Instead he looked tired and subdued.

'It's bloody depressing really,' he said, 'but then intelligence so often is.'

'I thought it was marvellous,' said Kieran, knowing how insincere that sounded. 'Really,' he added, making it worse. 'I know it sounds like a naive thing to say, but I've never been more struck by how contemporary Shakespeare can seem.'

'Quite so, my dear,' said Bertram absently; he was mostly concerned with extricating himself from his seat. 'Do we need to go somewhere to eat? Or just find a quiet drink?'

'Oh, a drink'll be fine.' Kieran was in fact ravenously hungry, but he knew that Bertram disliked late evening meals and would have fed himself amply during the day.

'Take me somewhere quiet and unliterary then.'

Kieran smiled. The idea that he knew West End bars better than a famous publisher who'd lived and worked here all his life was a quite unpremeditated piece of kind flattery.

'All right,' he said, as they emerged onto Charing Cross Road. 'Straight or, you know, the other thing?'

'I really don't mind as long as it sells alcohol and doesn't make a noise.'

Kieran thought of the Lamb and Flag, but somehow that belonged to Clive - and Clive's Kieran - so he steered them instead into a little pub in Monmouth Street which had somehow escaped yuppification. There was even room for them to sit with their drinks.

'Of course,' said Bertram, as if continuing a discussion he'd been having silently with himself, 'Shakespeare had some tremendous advantages. He wasn't for one thing inhibited by that ridiculous nineteenth century idea of character which still buggers up writers today. Dickens has a lot to answer for there, I'm afraid. Shakespeare could let his people move in and out of different kinds of focus, and even walk in and out of the action - take Thersites for example. And apart from that there's this extraordinary even-handedness: intellectual, sexual, moral. There are no taboos, no simple judgements. He even loves his villains. My dear, he *especially* loves his villains. Look at Macbeth. A man who kills his king, has his best friend murdered, and is happy to exterminate half the Scottish people to hang on to his crown. A shit. An absolute shit. And then look how we sympathise with him in those big speeches in Act Five: he gets all our emotional support. Just like Achilles. Same sort of thing. Unspeakable actions, and yet.... Though I suppose Achilles is slightly special.'

'Yes, I'd imagine someone must have made a case for it being a gay play.'

'No doubt.' Bertram snorted derisively. 'I'm afraid what it is is a queer play, and that's not altogether a bad thing. That's partly what I meant by even-handedness. He doesn't stack the odds in anyone's favour to start with. He shows you people at their worst and still persuades you to love them. It's a very rare kind of talent.

'That's why I was never keen on all that stuff about "positive images". Oh, I know it was well meant, but the trouble is that positive images tend not to convince. We're really not terribly interested in nice people. I'll tell you who the nicest guy in *Troilus and Cresssida* is. Antenor. I bet you can't even remember which one he was. No, we're interested in complicated good-and-evil people who turn out to have souls. Ah yes, souls. That *was* a little unkind.'

'You mean I'm not like Cressida after all?'

'No, my dear,' said Bertram. 'You're far prettier.' It wasn't an answer, and Bertram plainly didn't intend it to be. Then he seemed to relent. 'In point of fact, I still believe that you have got a soul. How about another drink?'

Kieran went to the bar, noting with weary familiarity that the barman was one of those bullocky little Irish boys who seemed to be everywhere this summer. They disputed sparringly over the ridiculous price of crinkle-cut crisps.

'You never miss a chance, do you, dear?' said Bertram when he returned with the drinks.

'I was arguing about the price of crisps,' replied Kieran, furious because it was true.

'That's another strange thing about Shakespeare.'

'The price of crisps?'

'No, the fact that although he seems to have been an exceptionally litigious man, there's one subject he hardly ever mentions, except in the rather coarse exception of *The Merchant of Venice*.'

'Which is?'

'Money. Of course there are good reasons for that. For one thing, the plays are to such an extent populated by great personages who can't be seen counting their coppers. For another, wealth or the lack of it didn't really become a central theme for writers until the development of the novel as a fully-fledged literary form - in other words, until the rise of industrial capitalism. Strange, all the same. You'd think the ordinary people in the plays and in the audience would have had a practical interest in coinage other than all those bawdy jokes about French crowns and so forth.

'However, you're letting me ramble again, my dear. On the whole I approve of people not talking about money, so I don't want you to say anything when I tell you I'm going to give you some. It's here somewhere.' Bertram fumbled in his inside jacket pocket and produced a rather crumpled white envelope. 'Now I want you to pay this in tomorrow morning. It's a cheque for quite a useful amount. You don't have to open it now - I don't particularly want you to know at this moment the price I've put on your head. Or anywhere else.' Bertram gave a brief helpless giggle.

Kieran suddenly remembered those childhood occasions - birthdays and Christmases - when his mother would give him a Book Token. There were all those agonising little delays - not opening it with undue haste, pausing to admire the design on the card, pretending to read the inscription inside - when all he really wanted to know was 'How much?' He guiltily felt much the same now. 'Thank you,' he said as gravely as he could manage. 'But why?'

'Why what?' Bertram was putting on his mock-cantankerous act. 'Why give it to you? Because I'm old and it's sitting in the bank and you need it and if you waste it that's your bloody look-out. Why here and now? Because I find the idea of slipping you a cheque at home vaguely distasteful and because I wanted to do it somewhere where's there's absolutely no point in making a great emotional scene of it. Now put it carefully into whatever passes for a pocket in those lemon-peel things of yours. Pay it in tomorrow. You never know, I might change my mind.'

* * *

Some time had passed since Clive last looked at *The Radical Urge*. He had instead been watching the shadow of his

76

own house creep gradually over the top storey and roof of the house opposite. On the apex of the roof, a pigeon on sentry-duty had been pacing neurotically back and forth, squinting in all directions for no very obvious purpose. Apart from this trifling distraction, Clive felt vaguely unwell, as he had done for so much of the summer. It had begun with a metallic taste, a deep yellow tongue, and a general sense of lethargy, at which point he had decided it was hepatitis; during a brief interlude of blisters around his groin he had toyed with genital herpes; and when virulent indigestion set in he found himself unable to choose between stomach cancer and duodenal ulcer. This evening he felt itchy as well as idle. He always felt itchy when Kieran had been around for the weekend. Once it had been crabs, but usually it was just a reflex.

There was, in any case, a problem with *The Radical Urge*, which was that it had been put together by a bunch of ologists. Clive had the artist's inevitable sneering contempt for people who wrote about anything ending in -ology, simply because of the wilful damage they insisted on inflicting on the language. They invented dialects which were unmeaningful because unmemorable, and strangely the problem seemed to become more rather than less acute as they moved voraciously towards literature: after years of half-heartedly trying, Clive still couldn't decide what, for instance, 'semiotic' actually meant - or what it signified. The sociologist author of the chapter which was strewn over his desk had the infuriating Teutonic habit of shunting words together as if he were building up a train of goods wagons: 'cryptopsycho-sexuality' he had uttered before Clive flung him down in fury. Since Clive's own notion of English prose was founded, reverently if fallibly, on that noble plain lucidity which ran from Jane Austen through to Forster and Isherwood, he found this sort of stuff almost impossible to manage. He wondered what Jane Austen would have made of it all, and felt he probably knew. 'Let other pens dwell on guilt and misery,' she would have written, as indeed she had.

Clive turned his attention to his first love, *Pendulum*. His plans for the 'After London' issue were beginning to shape up quite nicely. Almost everyone he'd contacted so far was eager to contribute: those he thought of as exiles - writers and artists who'd forsaken the capital to settle mostly in East Anglia or the West Country - were proving particularly keen to register their sense that urban culture was falling apart, presumably because they were no longer around to shore it up. Even dear old Graham Wagstaff, who lived in a steep almost Mediterranean street at Hatherleigh in Devon, and who never ventured further east than Exeter, wanted to pronounce on London's troubles. A number of Clive's London-based literary friends would write on why they wanted or intended to remove themselves from a malaise which had more to it than striking dustmen and thuggish policemen. And polymathic Karen would, he knew, produce a brain-storming essay combining feminism, environmentalism, and half a dozen other concepts. Isms were on the whole a good deal more manageable than ologies.

Clive felt - and was aware that he felt - the familiar, treacherous conviction that what he was doing with this issue might very slightly change the world. He had been driven for as long as he could remember by this obsessional and always disappointed faith in the published word. At school, editing a subversive sixth-form magazine had almost cost him his A levels; at university, he had overcome his social diffidence to hector and bully his way into the editorship of its arts magazine. This he had made fiercely his own, gaining for it a national reputation and for himself an indifferent degree. People said of him then as now, 'He's a marvellous editor' - and all along he knew that, yes, it was true, but it carried a usually unspoken codicil: 'Pity he never made it as a writer or artist himself, though.' But there it was: he loved being the means, the agent who selected and shaped and presented to the public work which other editors were too dim or too businesslike to accept. And he wanted, in a perfectly sincere and modest way, a better world: not the vague impractical hippie vision he'd fleetingly embraced in the late sixties along with people like Jeremy Barnes, but a more cultivated, less acquisitive place in which people would be nourished by the available good things - books, music, pictures, plants, wine. When caught in a traffic jam he'd find himself stupidly turning up Radio 3 not simply to drown the loathsome pop music drifting in from an adjacent car but in a naively educative spirit: one day, perhaps, someone would lean across and ask, 'What station's that, then?' It hadn't happened yet.

So, working fitfully on *Pendulum*, he watched the roofs of the vandalised world from his second-floor window. The noise of cars and radios, the sound of irrascible human voices, and the stench of uncollected rubbish floated up to him. 'You'll do as you're fucking well told,' said a paternal voice evidently to a three-year-old. Suffocation seemed almost preferable to this continued assault on the senses, so he closed the window, drew the blinds and put on a record. Up here, he had only vinyl - the CD player and discs were in the living-room - but that limitation had its own nostalgic rewards. He chose Finzi's *Clarinet Concerto*, happy in the knowledge that this piece, wonderful in itself, could be followed by the perfect miniature *Eclogue for Piano and String Orchestra* from the other side. He'd heard the *Clarinet Concerto* at a Prom, maybe fifteen years ago, and immediately embarked on his Finzi collection. This recording had appeared at roughly the same time: Clive remembered a review which began, 'Finzi was the last composer to sing of the English countryside'; and, despite the hint of journalistic sentimentality, there was a truth there which he wanted to pursue.

Never had he more urgently felt the need for simple fresh air. Here, in the fag-end of a London summer, was the last place he'd find it. It wasn't that he was tired of the city: he still liked, and up to a point still needed, the pubs and bars, the theatres and galleries, the inexhaustible moving exhibition of new anonymous faces. What he could no longer stand was the mixture filling the spaces in-between, all the uncouth dirt and noise. Leaving Finzi to his pastoral musing for a few moments, Clive went to the bathroom to throw some water over his face. The tap choked, gurgled, and emitted a spluttering rusty stream the colour of very unhealthy piss. He remembered a loudspeaker van squawking unintelligibly about something a while back and guessed that this time it must have been the water company. Eventually the flow cleared and Clive splashed it over himself, but it still smelled vaguely tainted and he felt less clean than he had before. The time was getting on. He'd better change into a clean shirt and go to the pub at the end of the *Concerto*; he'd save the *Eclogue* for later.

As he carefully closed the street-door behind him, he noticed an unfamiliar car, an old Jaguar, parked further down Salisbury Road. He registered it with the paranoid attention to detail which noted too that his own car, a shabbily undistinguished Volkswagen, was still where he'd parked it. A cheerful black youth wearing shorts and a harlequin-patterned sports shirt came hurtling down the pavement towards him, dribbling a football between the rubbish-sacks. 'Hiya man,' he said, 'you doin' all right?' Otherwise the street was deserted and so, when he reached it, was the Clarendon, except for a few solitaries posted at contemplative intervals along the bar. The weekday regulars were either on holiday, he assumed, or they'd just returned from holiday without any money left - while the weekend crowd often seemed to vanish on a Monday, catching up with its washing, nursing its hangover, or counting its pennies. Gwylim was nowhere to be seen but Alex, unbidden, pulled him a pint.

'One for yourself?'

'Thanks, Clive. I'll have a half. Two pounds for cash.' Even his weekend zaniness had faded.

The other faces at the bar were unfamiliar, except perhaps for the one furthest from him. Despite the self-effacingly plain casual clothes, he looked like the blond boy in the leather jacket from Saturday afternoon. He also looked like the younger of the two policemen from outside Tesco's on Friday. Clive stared at him, and he stared back, almost as if he wanted Clive to note his presence. There was probably nothing in it, apart from fruitless confusion. If he were a leather boy in civvies he might be worth chatting up; if he were an off-duty policeman he'd best be avoided; if he were both - well, it was possible, but it didn't bear thinking about.

'All on your own, you poor old sod?' Claude had oozed through the door and swayed up to the bar beside him. 'Put one in the pump for him and give me a large gin and tonic, Alex, there's a dear. Not too many of them cloudy ice cubes though. You could get typhoid from the ice in this bar, I shouldn't wonder. God alone knows what you could get from that bloody beer.'

'Thanks, Claude. A hangover, perhaps.'

'A hangover? *Hang*over? Bloody hell, I've never had one of them. Never stopped drinking for long enough.' He laughed too loudly. 'Well I must say we've got a lively bunch in here tonight. Tell you what, I've just been in the Red Lion and that's a fucking morgue as well. Three senile old goats playing darts and a couple of puffed-up tarts at the bar pretending to be hairdressers. I said to them, I said, "How many stylists have you got working in this so-called salon of yours?" "Five," one of them says, all puffed-up and proud. "All right then, not counting YTS, how many?" "Two." "Two," I says, "and you call *that* a salon?" Ignorant bloody bitches. I think I might have upset them.'

Clive tried to watch without Claude noticing as the blond boy slipped out of the bar, but of course there wasn't a chance.

'Who's that then? Another friend of yours?'

'No, complete stranger,' said Clive. 'You don't happen to know him?'

'Not bloody likely. Looks like filth to me. You can tell by the way they carry their arses. It's all part of their training at Hendon. At least, training's what they call it: more like gang rape, if they're lucky. Alex, put some more gin in this. It looks like a bloody Fox's Glacier Mint in the bottom of that glass.'

'I'll get it.'

'Well I won't try and stop you. You'll only get temperamental.'

'No I wouldn't, but I'm still going to buy you a drink. It's been a trying day, but I'm starting to feel almost relaxed.'

'That's a bad sign. I don't trust you when you're not neurotic. What the bloody hell's this? More friends of yours?'

The three skinheads marched so purposefully across to the bar that even Alex's composure seemed momentarily disturbed before his face settled back into its habitual expression of ironic enquiry. But they ordered their lagers with surprising civility before taking them to a table by the window.

'He'll have to change that tape now,' said Claude. The machine was playing one of Gwylim's worst-hits-of-the-sixties compilations. 'Here, Alex, put on something more appropriate to the clientele. "Land of Hope and Glory" or "Jerusalem". Or perhaps "You'll Never Walk Alone".'

'"You'll Never Walk Again" more likely,' said Clive quietly. 'Do watch it, Claude.'

'Watch it? What for? You're back to your old neurotic self all of a sudden. I don't know, everyone's so bloody jittery these days. Take my advice. Treat the world with benign contempt and it won't know what to make of you. Don't let the bastards think they've got you sorted out. Anyway, I'm off. Needs must, whatever that means. You've still got a drink in the pump, remember.' He rose unsteadily from his stool and tottered across to the skinheads on his way to the door. 'Goodnight, boys,' he said, patting one of them on the head so weightily that he crumpled downwards in his chair. 'Lovely texture,' said Claude and went on, turning in the doorway to take a long theatrical bow. The skinheads laughed amiably. Maybe there was no harm in them after all.

Nevertheless, one of them, the one who'd ordered the drinks, looked familiar: wasn't he one of those who'd been cluttering up Craven Street on Saturday? But skinheads, for Clive, had a kind of oriental sameness about them, and he couldn't be sure. In any case, this mania for recognition was in danger of getting out of hand.

'Ready for that pint?' asked Alex.

'Yes. Thanks.'

'You okay?'

'Yes, fine. It's just that I keep thinking people look like other people.'

Alex considered this for a moment as he pulled the pint. 'Who do I look like then?'

'James Dean.'

For a moment Alex brightened visibly.

'After the car crash,' said Clive.

'Thanks a lot. You could easily pass for Marlon Brando yourself. In *The Godfather*. Or Godmother.'

'Bitch. Bit quiet this evening, isn't it?'

'Not quiet enough for me,' said Alex with a nod towards the skinheads.

'Mustn't be judgemental. They've been less nuisance than Claude so far.'

'He's charmed. Either that or he's so far gone that no-one's going to bother to smack him any more.'

'I actually rather like him. He may be in a rut but it's a rut all of his own. And he's no fool.'

Though that, Clive reflected, as Alex wafted away down the bar, was exactly what he was: the Shakespearian fool, the melancholic court jester. Clive wondered whether Claude was pining away inside, and decided that he probably was.

A few more desultory drinkers had wandered in - fugitives from *Panorama* and repeats on television - but Clive was struck by how thin and colourless the Monday evening crowd seemed to be, as he furtively appraised it in the mirror behind the bar. This evening, the Clarendon had reverted to its old orthodox self, an unexceptional pub in a generally respectable London suburb, its clientele readily definable only in negatives: they were not successful family men, who had moved out to executive homes in posh commuter villages near Letchworth; nor affluent yuppies, who had moved in to high-rent low-rise

83

fashionable pads nearer the city; nor the happily uncommitted, who had simply moved on to numerous airy elsewheres. They were people, in fact, of various yet irrefutable middlingness. And three skinheads. And Clive.

He was still not happy about the skinheads so, having checked with the mirror that they still had a reasonable amount of lager in their glasses, he decided to drink up and go. He waved his farewell to Alex who, as if by instinct, didn't call out his customary 'Cheers, Clive' but merely returned a silent wave, and slipped as unobtrusively as possible out of the bar.

The night was oppressive, still and overcast, cushioning down on London as if to stifle its breath. Where air should have been, there were the pungent exhalations of chip shops and takeaways; and, instead of moon and stars, the only light came from sulky amber streetlamps and the tacky glitzy windows of video shops. Clive walked softly and steadily, pausing to look at uninteresting windows, until he was fairly certain that he wasn't being followed, then doubled back, crossed the street and headed down the wide alleyway towards Salisbury Road. He had reached the ornamental gaslamp midway along it when a voice from behind, cockney but courteous, stopped him.

'Excuse me,' it said, 'Mr Greenslade.'

The speaker was the lager-buying skinhead, flanked on either side by his two friends, like aircraft flying in V-formation. Clive thought about making a dash for it, but there was no point: they were younger and fitter than he was, they could catch him easily if they wanted, and he had no wish to end up flattened against his own front door. Besides, an obstinate defiance told him that he wasn't going to start running away from complete strangers on his home territory.

'Yes,' he said with absurd civility, 'What can I do for you?'

'Oh no,' said the skinhead, 'it's a question of what I can do for you.' He looked at each of his mates for approval, and Clive sensed that he was in for a studied performance.

'First of all, I was asked to give you a message. Or credentials, you might say. Just so's you know that we know.' He handed Clive a stiff buff envelope. 'Hang on to it, whatever happens. You might find it enlightening. Now secondly, do you think we could move a bit out of this glare? There must be a slightly less public place for our chat. After all, we don't want to upset your neighbours.'

Clive found himself shifting involuntarily into an unlit corner of the high-walled alleyway.

'Don't worry, we're not planning on hurting you. As long as you're not daft enough to try and leg it. In that case' - with almost balletic precision the two henchmen produced Stanley knives from their pockets and flashed the blades at Clive - 'we'd have to think again. But you're not daft. You know a friendly warning when you see one. Speaking of which, we had to give a little warning to that ace footballer friend of yours. It wasn't in the script, but it seemed a good idea. Dean's idea, really. Tell the man, Dean.'

'Yeah,' said the right-hand skinhead, with measured enthusiasm. 'We took your black mate for a little ride up the multi-storey. While you was downing your first pint, this was. It was for his own good, really, warning him to stay clear of lefty poofs like you. We didn't hurt him bad - nothing special, like. He'll walk. Come to that, he fucking *ran* down them stairs when we let him go.' Dean smirked. 'Funny limp, though.'

Clive was wondering with a mixture of fascination and terror what Dean's notion of something 'special' might be when the first skinhead spoke again.

'Anyway, your black brother won't be going to the police, will he? I think we got that into his golliwog's head. Any nuisance from him, and he'll be fitted up for a nice little drugs bust, no trouble. We're quite often on the side of law and order, see? Apart from which, I expect Dean'll have his dick fried for breakfast. With or without tomatoes. Unless he decides to grill it instead. Remember that prat we did with the toaster, Dean?'

Dean licked his lips for a moment in silent recollection: he was evidently the tame maniac of the three. 'Didn't seem so keen on popping up after that, did he?'

'So that's it really. Just a friendly warning. Get your arse out of London and stop upsetting our mates in high places. They really don't appreciate it, sunshine. They get cross, and then they get unfriendly. So if we have to see you again, I'm very much afraid it'll be a rubber gloves job with the Stanley.' Dean obligingly made a skewering movement with his blade. 'You see? Major surgery, in your case.

'There's only one last thing. You see, we have to get away, just like they do on tv, right?' Abruptly the talkative skinhead, Wayne, snatched the buff envelope from Clive's hand, and it fell on the ground between them. 'Now, Mr Greenslade, I told you to take care of that.' Thinking with half his mind that he was falling for an obvious trick, Clive stooped to pick up the envelope. The first boot hit him in the shoulder, the second in the ribs, the third - Dean's, how did he know? - expertly and lingeringly in the balls. He crouched, curled round the precious envelope, as the kicks, painful but aimed perhaps with a certain judicious restraint, came at him.

'That'll do. Friendly warning. Now don't go squealing to anyone, 'cause we're sure to hear about it. And don't move till we're well out of sight unless you want some personal amputation. Right? Dean? Do your stuff.'

The third, speechless skinhead leant forward towards Clive, grabbing him by the hair and gesturing with his knife. 'Open wide,' he said.

'Golden shower time,' said Dean, unzipping his jeans. 'Hope you like warm secondhand lager.'

When Clive got to his feet a few minutes later, he was completely calm: it was, he knew, that scary calm which arrives on the other side of panic. He walked briskly and almost painlessly out of the alley and across Salisbury Road, looking straight ahead of him: he didn't want to catch even a distant glimpse of anyone he knew. There was a football in the gutter outside his front door, and on the door itself were the words QUEER NIGGER FUCKER AIDS CARRIER. Clive wiped his forearm cross them and they smeared into a blur; they weren't indellible. The skinheads had in their way been careful - it was just a warning. He unlocked the door, thankful above all that Cath was away on holiday: he couldn't have handled her reactions to the graffiti nor her sympathetic ministrations to his hurt self. He half-expected something to have been pushed through his letter-box, but there was nothing: they had of course communicated with him more directly. He carefully locked the front door and ran upstairs to his flat. As soon as he'd closed the flat door behind him he rushed to the bathroom and turned on the bath-taps as far as they'd go. They gurgled and protested and at last began to fill the bath. He tipped in half a bottle of green herbal nonsense. The splashing gradually modulated to a soft bubbly patter.

As Clive began to remove his clothes pain, or perhaps the memory of pain, returned to him. So, as he took off his soaking shirt, did something more disconcerting, a distinct erotic charge: he wouldn't have predicted that being pissed on by a skinhead would have excited him, but there it was, in retrospect at least. That was the trouble with sex: it had no respect for gravity or absurdity, and it found the juxtaposition of the two wholly irresistible. Clive gave his shirt a reflective sniff, and got rid of the rest of his clothes. There were lurid red marks which would probably metamorphose into bruises on his shoulders and ribs. The bath was now as full as it would ever be, of bubbles mostly, so he lowered himself gently into it. Contact with the water immediately identified the locations of pain and almost immediately soothed them. His body started to feel better. He immersed his head in the foam and hoped that when he emerged he would smell more like a herb garden than a urinal.

After a while he got out and very cautiously dried himself. Flinging his clothes in the laundry-basket, he went into his bedroom and put on clean jeans and a t-shirt. Then he poured himself a large scotch, collected the envelope which was still lying unopened on the bathroom floor, and went up to his studio to think.

At times of crisis the studio, with all its purposeful clutter, always seemed a more helpful place than the living-room. He had already decided that there was nothing he could usefully do about the black boy. Clive didn't know his name, had only the haziest notion of where he might live, and couldn't in any case see how his intervention would do other than add to the distress and confusion of an apparently senseless racist attack. His own treatment made him fairly certain that the boy wouldn't have been badly hurt, and he took a little comfort from that. There remained the envelope, which he had treated as if it were an unexploded bomb, knowing that whatever it contained would probably demand a considered response and a stiff drink. Sitting at his studio desk, he took a large gulp of whisky and ripped open the envelope.

It contained three polaroid prints and three folded photocopies. The polaroids showed Clive, laden with shopping, emerging from Tesco's on Friday; Clive and Kieran parading down the Embankment on Saturday afternoon; Clive and Kieran leaving the house in Salisbury Road, sometime on Sunday. Two of the photocopies were rather smudgy reproductions of a younger naked Kieran from the pages of a gay magazine; the third was the article from *Pendulum* on the Villiers Street incident. That connection was now clear enough, but it was hard to see what else the package proved, except that someone had been watching and checking and researching - probably someone official. It didn't really amount to a threat or blackmail. It was, in fact, just what Wayne had said: credentials.

What Clive couldn't determine was whether, or to what extent, this might constitute a danger to Kieran. It might be as well to phone him, though all he was likely to convey would be self-pity for his done-over limbs. He dialled the number and let it ring, and was almost relieved when there was no reply: Kieran was probably out post-theatre boozing with old Philpotts or else tucking him up in bed in

88

Earl's Court. Clive looked around the room for reassurance or even for revenge. That policeman who'd been in collusion with the muggers: could he have been the one from the pub, from the march, from outside the supermarket? What was his name? Clive reached into the filing cabinet and soon found the original report. Sergeant Andrew Symes. Was it worth it? After London, it might be worth it, but right now it was reassurance he needed most. 'Cryptopsychosexuality,' scowled the typescript on his desk. *'Eclogue for Piano and String Orchestra,'* smiled the record label. He put the record on and bathed in the music, but by the time the short piece ended he was slumped over his desk, fast asleep.

FIVE

After some trivial agonising, Jeremy had decided to take Bill out to lunch at The Ship. There were disadvantages: it meant a fifteen-minute drive, and the old man would make a huge, self-indulgent fuss about the difficulty of getting in and out of Jeremy's venerable Triumph Vitesse, in the back of which he would contrive to leave his walking-stick (ample proof, it seemed to Jeremy, that he didn't need the bloody thing in the first place); and the drive would inescapably take them through Leiston, a place which seldom failed to depress him and in some opaque way trouble his conscience. Against this had to be set a decisive number of advantages. He really didn't want to cook for Bill, who would easily become boozily soporific if they stayed in one place, and felt more inclined to reserve his culinary skills for Clive's promised visit later in the week. He loved Dunwich - to say nothing of The Ship - and hoped to tempt Bill at least to the cliff, if not to the beach. And, above all, he knew that, since he no longer drove, Bill was almost childishly delighted to be taken anywhere outside Aldeburgh, despite the protestations and the recalcitrant walking-stick.

In the event, many of Jeremy's predictions were mistaken. Bill didn't grumble about the car, and Leiston didn't spread its usual stultifying gloom. Instead, quite unprompted, Bill offered his own explanation of its customary emotional effect. 'Troublesome place,' he said. 'I'm afraid it's because the ugliness offends us, but then we're even more offended at ourselves for having been offended in the first place. It brings out all our arty-farty insecurity. But I don't think we'd swap.' They were approaching the redundant level-crossing. 'Look at that,' he continued, gesturing to his left, 'all split up into piddling little units now. But I can remember when as

91

Garrett Engineering it was the only *real* employer in the area. The Garretts did a lot of good, actually. God knows why they also had to build a replica of Coketown round their factory.'

Having settled into the role of an eccentric guidebook, Bill continued in the same vein for the rest of the journey. At Westleton he announced: 'There's a remarkable clematis-grower here, but I've never succeeded in finding him.' And at Dunwich Heath: 'There used to be signs round here which said "Beware of Adders", but I could never quite decide what in practice that meant. I suppose you have to make a lot of noise to scare them off. Sing rousing patriotic songs, that kind of thing.'

It was only just midday when they arrived at Dunwich, and the village seemed relatively deserted. 'I suppose,' said Bill, 'we'd better go and have a look at that bloody tombstone. See if John Brinkley Easey's gone over the edge yet.' He climbed out of the car with considerable sprightliness, and they set off towards the cliff. They were halfway along the overgrown path before Bill said, 'Damnit, I've left my stick in your car.' He gave an impish grin. 'Daresay I'll manage,' he added.

They looked out from the cliff-top at the placid dishwater-coloured sea, flecked occasionally by vivid patches of brightness. On the beach below, a group of children were chucking pebbles into it, doing their bit for coastal erosion. The solitary headstone of John Brinkley Easey was still in its place, surrounded by a small sand-pit in a surprisingly grassy part of the cliff-top.

'I almost think the old bugger's going to outlast me,' grumbled Bill. 'I'd always fondly imagined that he'd be the first to go. Do you think I should give him a push?' The old man's enthusiasm for the idea seemed momentarily so satanic that Jeremy had a clear image of him heaving the stone over the brink, probably onto the children playing beneath the cliff.

'No, I think perhaps not,' he said, looking once more out to sea.

'Your sort of place this, isn't it? Bells tolling under the

92

waves, things like that.'

Jeremy laughed. 'Yes, I love the sense of successive pasts overlaid on each other, but I really don't go for all the sentimental trappings. Come on, let's head back. The pub'll be filling up.'

It was. Although overcast and a Tuesday, it was also the holiday season, and as usual a quite improbable number of people had found their way through the network of narrow lanes to this place which no longer existed. They both ordered fish, because that is what The Ship is rightly famous for, and Bill even deserted his customary gin-and-tonic in favour of Adnams' bitter. By putting on a cunning and convincing show of elderliness he miraculously secured them a table; he further secured for himself a surprisingly stately chair, leaving Jeremy to perch on one of the solid little barrrels dotted about the bar. At the next table, an earnest bunch of walkers bound for Southwold had just discovered from a crumpled map that there was a river in the way, and decided to get drunk instead. Bill, as they ate, seemed to forget that he didn't want to be rediscovered.

'I suppose,' he said, 'it might be possible to get one or two of my novels back into print. In paperback. I'm really not sure if they're worth reviving. Have you read any of them?'

'Only *Unreal City* - and the poems, of course. You've always refused to lend me the others.'

'Have I really? Well, I can't say that *Unreal City* is my favourite. The title's an allusion to Eliot, of course - that image of the crowds crossing the Thames, all those people whom death had "undone", that was my starting- point for the whole thing. It's very much of its moment, but that's the best you can say for it.'

'What about the others, then? And anyway, why did you stop?'

'I stopped,' Bill said slowly, 'because I had a row with my publisher and I simply got fed up with the whole tiresome business. Well, perhaps not simply. The publisher was a rather tedious old queer - sorry, but he was

- called Bertram Philpotts. We were actually extremely good friends for many years, until he quite absurdly took exception to something in one of my books: he made out that it would be libellous, or something, whereas what he really meant was that his prissy little publishing house, Whiting & Hammond, didn't want to touch anything which would set the teacups rattling. We had quite a famous row about it, in public too. I'm afraid' - Bill lowered his voice - 'it ended with me storming out of a rather famous literary pub saying, "Whiting & Hammond are a load of shit, and you're finished." And that, as you may imagine, rather upset our friendship.'

'I can imagine that it might,' said Jeremy.

Bill munched happily for a moment or two. 'This is excellent, by the way,' he said. 'Though there was more to it than that. This is, of course, off the record, as they say. I was having an affair with a wonderful Italian woman called Francesca Bellorini - I liked to put it about that she was a countess, though in fact she was just a bloody good cook. Anyway, Francesca had a brother, Raffaeli, who was every bit as charming and several years younger, and naturally enough Bertram met him at one of my parties - or one of his, I really can't remember which. He was immediately bewitched, buggered and be-whatnotted by the boy: sent him presents every other day, wrote endless letters. Bertram liked to make out that he was totally callous in his affairs, but he was a sentimental old thing, especially when he couldn't fully possess what he wanted. Raffaeli lapped up the presents for a while, but he wasn't having Bertram. It was Francesca, though, who finally wouldn't stand for it. I think she threatened Bertram quite unpleasantly - this is the early fifties, remember - and that didn't do much for our professional relationship either.'

'And that was when you left London? You inherited a house in Tunbridge Wells, didn't you?'

'Well, yes and no. It always sounded a sufficiently ludicrous story, but the truth was more ludicrous still. Francesca and I certainly went to Tunbridge Wells. In fact, we ran a junk shop. Quite near the Pantiles, just off the

94

High Street in one of the steep little alleys near Mount Sion. I'm almost ashamed to say it, but it was the most marvellous fun. It was called Francesca's, and for all the world knew I was just an eccentric lodger who helped out. I had Hall's lovely secondhand bookshop just down the hill from me, Goulden and Curry for new books and civilised music, some wonderful gin-palace pubs and total anonymity. Every so often I'd nip into London to see what was happening in the antique markets, and sometimes I'd pop into some of the Soho literary pubs just to remind people that I was still alive. But after a while I decided that they might just as well think I was dead.'

'And so you vanished completely?'

'Yes, I suppose I did. Francesca left me, of course, and as a solo junk-shop proprietor I began rather to lose my enthusiasm. So in the late fifties I came here.' Bill chuckled reflectively. 'I did go back to Tunbridge Wells a few years later to see what had become of Francesca's. They'd turned it into a shop selling trendy men's clothes - very bright, cheap stuff, and way ahead of Aldeburgh at the time. I couldn't believe it: Tunbridge Wells had become fashionable. Anyway, I went in, and to the astonishment of the very beautiful young man who was running it - he was all long hair and beads, and there was a tape of a sitar playing - I actually bought some clothes. I particularly remember a deep purple shirt with a huge collar. Aldeburgh had seen nothing like it. Unfortunately, almost all the colour came out the first time I washed it.'

'How did you make a living then? I mean, I don't want to pry or anything, but you can't have had that much stashed away, and as far as I know you didn't open a junk shop in Aldeburgh.'

'I did in fact have a fair bit. At that time property in Kent was worth a good deal more than property in Suffolk. But you're right. I did almost anything: freelance odds and ends, selling, a bit of reviewing. I ran the bar in one of the hotels for a while, but I'm afraid it didn't agree with me. I spent an absolutely mournful few months traipsing round East Suffolk trying to sell magazine subscriptions on commission. And I did work for the Coastguard Service for quite a time.'

'So that's where the other part of the legend comes in - the bit about becoming a lighthouse-keeper.'

'Yes, exactly, it was just like the Tunbridge Wells thing. In both cases I knew just about enough of the subject to put on a convincing show if it should ever come to that. So the world, if it cared, could imagine that I'd inherited a house in a vaguely preposterous place and then become an eccentric reclusive lighthouse-keeper. Quite crazy, of course, but then the world didn't care. I wonder,' he added, eyeing the next table, 'what that cherry pie is like. Do you think we might find out?'

'I'll go to the Galley and get us some,' said Jeremy. 'Cream or ice-cream? I think the cream tends to be that squidgy stuff, but the ice-cream is probably home-made.'

'You *are* well-informed,' said Bill, with real admiration, 'and of course I defer to your judgement. Shall I get us some more beer in the meantime?'

'Yes, as long as our claim to the table's clearly staked. Just a half for me. I'm driving. And you're going to give me some more material for my "After London" piece, remember.'

When Jeremy returned with two plates of cherry pie and ice-cream, he found that Bill had discovered someone he knew at the bar: there probably wasn't a pub in Suffolk whose bar didn't contain someone he knew. Nevertheless, their table, occupied by plates and glasses with Bill's coat flung possessively over the chair, hadn't been taken.

'Frightfully interesting chap,' said Bill, with every appearance of meaning it. 'Can't remember what he does....' It was at moments like this, Jeremy noticed, that Bill's class, an intuitive sense of good manners which his famously wilful rudeness couldn't wholly obliterate, showed up. 'This looks splendid,' he said, of but also to the pie.

'Let's hope it tastes as good.'

'I'm sure it will. You know, it's odd sitting here, of all places, thinking about your "After London" idea in the remains of the great lost city of East Anglia. Eleven (is it?) or twelve churches under the sea. Now that really is the death of a city.'

'Do you know, I hadn't even seen the connection until now. How incredibly dim of me. It must have been pure instinct brought us here.'

'That, or beer and food,' said Bill.

'That, *and* beer and food.'

'Perhaps. I sometimes wonder whether you don't think too hard - I'm damned if I'm going to say you work too hard - and so confuse your big ideas with too much piddling detail. You need to broaden your horizons.'

'Oh,' said Jeremy, 'my horizons are boundless. It's just that sometimes there's nothing on them.'

When, driving back, Jeremy took the Thorpeness road to Aldeburgh, Bill beamed his approval. 'It sounds terribly silly,' he said, 'but I judge people by which route they take at this point. The little stretch of coast road from Thorpeness to Aldeburgh is so exhilarating, and so extraordinary. Have you ever considered why?'

'Well, it *is* invigorating, and it gets us home without all the suburban stuff inland, but there's another reason?'

'Oh yes,' said Bill, and then stopped as if, like Professor Godbole, he had not the slightest intention of divulging it. 'It's very simple really,' he went on at last. 'It's just that it's the only piece of coast road between Felixstowe and Lowestoft. All the other roads point at the sea and then sheer off. It's most uncharacteristic of the North Sea to provide such an amenable stretch of coastline.'

Yes, thought Jeremy, and there were other attractions in the way that the surprisingly open seascape gave way to the happy contradictions of the town. To the right there was a sudden resortish flurry of Victorian hotels and a pompous little terrace, but even this couldn't take itself entirely seriously when confronted on the left with the boats and fishermen's huts and the perky Moot Hall. Carnival weekend was imminent, and the streets were already being decked with bunting, and in Crabbe Street outside the Cross Keys a man was watering tubs and hanging-baskets with profound though unsteady concentration. Jeremy parked the car off King Street and this time remembered to rescue Bill's walking-stick.

As they entered the house, Ben stirred from his midday snooze with a couple of half-hearted barks before dropping off again, apparently placated by the promise of a walk along the shore to Thorpeness at low tide. Soon, seated in Jeremy's small living-room with a large gin-and-tonic - he had with predictable haughtiness declined the offer of coffee - Bill began to talk about the death of cities.

'I really think that, whichever way you look at it, the collapse of urban culture had become inevitable by the late fifties. One reason, ironically enough, was that short of a nuclear war which would have wiped us all out, we seemed set for a period of prolonged peace in Europe. And that allowed people to start thinking in quite new ways about, if you like, re-engineering their world. They started to rationalise the idea of a city - whereas in fact the whole strength of a city, above all a capital city, is its marvellous cohesive irrationality, the bringing together of all sorts of disparate and incompatible things *only* because they share that sense of a centre.

'Covent Garden's a good example. Now when I left London, and for a good few years after that, Covent Garden meant two things. The best opera house in the country and the best wholesale fruit-and-veg market. So what have opera and greengrocery got in common, and don't say fruits? Absolutely bugger all, except for the sense of a centre. And that's why the place had such a special sense of cultural vitality. You had opera singers falling over barrow-boys and vice-versa - all right, you can snigger - in a way that was mutually enlightening and very good for both of them. And if you walked through the market when the day's business was done you had that extraordinary feeling of a great building resting, of enormous energies spent and empty spaces about to be reinhabited. I don't think I'm being sentimental, but I'm sure you don't get any of that now. What you've got is a constant fun-fair full of people who share the same

98

artificial expectations, the same cultural impoverishments, speak the same codes, and who therefore can't be expected to surprise each other in any very profound way. All they can do is to confirm the mirage of each other's existence. Mostly they're just airy nothings.

'That's part of it, that's one strand, but it's only one aspect of a much bigger problem. It's all to do with space and pressure and violence. Look at the tubes, the roads, the pavements - everywhere there's the same sense of overcrowding in an increasingly shabby, shoddy environment. Things like the King's Cross fire are both literal inevitabilities and metaphors for the greater disasters to come. Places like Covent Garden'll go up in flames in the end.'

'But surely,' Jeremy ventured, 'cities have always been crowded - always *over*crowded?'

'Well of course in one sense that's true, and you've only got to look at old prints or old newsreel to see it. But I think there are two differences. The first I'm not terribly sure about - I'm not an architect or an engineer after all - but it does seem to me that if you put large numbers of people into cities made of brick and granite they're less likely to come to grief than they are in places made of plastic and glass. That's not the main point, though. The main point is that the old crowds may have had a few stars in them but they were mostly men in bowler hats and women in sensible shoes. Nowadays there are too many stars. Look at any West End street and you'll see what I mean: they *all* want to be actors. And it won't bloody well work. Cities are theatre, after all, and in any theatre you've got to have more audience than actors. I suppose that's really what I meant by pressure: it's the wrong kind of pressure, the kind that builds up behind the actor's disguise, behind the mask. That has to be explosive in the end.'

'And violence? You mentioned violence.'

'Yes, it's almost the counterpart of disasters. Disasters are, after all, a kind of communal violence: they're if you like the spirit of the city avenging itself at random on a section of the community. Personal violence (and it hardly matters if it's yobs in the street or policeman in the cells) may be more complicated - for one thing it has a psychology in a way that a burning station or stadium doesn't - but it has one vital thing in common. Disasters and violence are both inarticulate. They happen when words have failed. They happen when different kinds of pressure have grown beyond words.'

'I've never heard you sound quite so seriously pessimistic.'

'I'm desolate. I think the late twentieth century city is a place where it's very hard to be articulate - at any rate, articulate in the certainty of being understood. And that of course is a moral issue. I don't mean "moral" in the weak, prissy, censorious sense, naturally. I mean that where language fails in its social context, it becomes impossible to debate or discuss or perhaps even think about the moral intricacies which should underpin even - or especially - our most outrageous actions. The city has become a place where it's very, very difficult to be *good*.' Bill shrugged and smiled with a kind of gloomy elation, like a North Sea sky. 'I'm glad I got out in time, glad that I can still function reasonably well, glad that I've got some space around me. But I suppose I've just truthfully answered, for the first time, the question "Why did you stop writing?". After all, the city that's busy destroying itself *was* my culture. Do you think it'll ever be possible in the future to teach children that "urban" and "urbane" come from the same root?'

'Yes, I've some small faith in cyclical regeneration. Maybe it'll come with the millenium.'

'Well, that *will* be after my time. At least I bloody well hope so. Has all that been taping? That red thing like an electronic barometer keeps going up and down.'

'It's fine. Would you like another drink?'

'A thin one, Jeremy, a very thin one. And where, by the way, do you stand in this argument?'

Jeremy tried to look thoughtful as he poured Bill's drink, but he felt blank. 'I suppose I stand aside from it, waiting to see what will happen. That's a terribly inadequate response, but right now I'm almost grateful to be stuck here. Though "stuck"'s wrong too - I chose to be here, and I'm not regretting it. It's people like Clive Greenslade I'm worried about. You're right about pressure. Anyway, he's coming here for a few days later in the week. You'll meet him.'

'Good. From what you've told me about him at various times, I've got a mental picture which is almost certainly wrong.'

'Why?'

'Because I've had to invent the rest. Can't kick the habit. I've had to give him physical details - I only know that he's your age and slightly less scruffy. He's got mousy hair and blue eyes.'

'North Sea grey, actually.'

'And I've had to invent a voice, and above all a past. It'll be interesting to see how he matches up. Of course, being an editor rather goes against him.'

'He doesn't seem very editorial to me.'

'Nor to me,' said Bill confidently. 'In fact, he seems like a man who thinks of life as a novel of which he's simultaneously author and hero, yes?'

'An unreliable narrator, certainly.'

'Then if he comes to the coast and doesn't return to the city, he's heading for his last page.'

* * *

As he sheered off from the crowd in St Martin's Lane, Kieran knew only that with what little money he had until he could draw on Bertram's cheque, with luck tomorrow, he was somehow going to get drunk. It wasn't quite self-destruction: it was self-obliteration, the temporary but complete removal to a region where failure, anxiety and despair could no longer hammer at him. Once he'd arrived there, it was true, accidents tended to happen. He'd pick up boys who would threaten or rob him - only last week some Jason or Justin had stolen his third Walkman, leaving

Kieran naked and sleepily pleading in bed next morning - but he very seldom actually got hurt. The tables in the alleyway outside the entrance to The Pit were already crowded with boys, some of whom Kieran cursorily acknowledged. He headed straight into the sudden gloom, down the pungent staircase, past the stacked crates, and through the glass doors into the bar. A wave of smoke, sweat and noise engulfed him, The Pet Shop Boys in what sounded like at least the fifteenth remix:

> Your life's a mystery,
> Mine is an open book.
> If I could read your mind,
> Maybe I'd take a look.
> I don't care,
> Baby, I'm not scared.

Another new barman poured him a pint of expensive fizzy bitter: they changed so frequently these days that he wondered whether their Pit t-shirts got washed between occupants. He looked around the dim, hazy room at the shrouded piano, the half-empty tables. It was early, still sunny outside, and the indoor crowd was relatively sparse; but Kieran didn't want sunlight, even though that was where the boys were. Here the customers were mostly solitary grey men, standing around waiting for something which probably wouldn't happen.

> What have you got to fight?
> What do you need to prove?
> You're always telling lies,
> And that's the only truth.
> I don't care,
> Baby, I'm not scared.

Only one figure caught his attention, the blond boy in the leather jacket whom he'd noticed on Saturday. ('Tonight the streets are full of actors, / I don't know why....') He was obviously a stranger here, maybe a visitor or tourist who'd overheard Kieran's deliberately emphatic reference to The Pit, and he was sitting alone at a table, attempting or pretending to read a Penguin copy of *The Swimming-Pool Library*. Kieran watched him, unsure but suspecting that

102

he was being watched in return, drinking his pint more rapidly than he'd intended. He'd need to be on his second drink before making a move. ('I'd go anywhere,' sang the insistent voice, 'Baby, I'm not scared.') The barman refilled his glass, and Kieran ambled across the room.

'I saw you on Saturday afternoon,' he said. 'Do you mind if I join you?'

The boy in the leather jacket gestured neutrally. Kieran sat down.

'It's a good novel, though I'm not sure about the ending.'

'I haven't got that far yet.'

'No, of course not.'

'Anyway,' he closed the book, 'I shouldn't get much further in this light. I only bought it to read on the tube.'

'Which line?'

'Piccadilly.'

'Good.' Kieran grinned. 'I thought all those extracts from the old man's diary were a bit boring too.'

'Yes.' The boy didn't want to talk about the book, which was obviously just a prop. That was all right then.

'I enjoyed Saturday,' said Kieran. 'It seemed all very civilised and peaceful. No easy copy for the tabloids, and no political capital for the old bitch.'

'Yes, you're right, it wasn't quite what I expected.' The boy stared at his lager with what seemed like a look of puzzled disapproval. Then he looked up at Kieran. 'Do you fancy a drink somewhere else?' he said. 'Maybe go west a bit? It's nearer my home. Then perhaps...?'

Kieran tried to look encouraging: the speech had come out with an effort which was rather charming in its awkwardness, engagingly at odds with the tight jeans and leather jacket.

'Listen, yes of course, but I've got to say I've very little cash on me. I'd feel guilty about scrounging off you all evening.'

'Oh that's okay.' Confidence abruptly seemed to resurface. 'I've just had a pay rise.'

'What do you do?'

'Just dull office work. At a warehouse in Hammersmith.

And you?'

'Much the same, when I can get it, or stand it. I'd like to be able to say I'm a writer. Fuck it, I'm actually on the dole. Resting, as an actor would say.'

'Never mind. I'll buy you a few drinks, and we can take it from there. What's your name, by the way?'

'Kieran,' said Kieran.

'Gary,' said the leather boy.

They clasped hands, and once again Kieran was aware of the discrepancy between Gary's self-assurance and uncertainty: the handshake was altogether conventional, the grasp more tentative than he'd anticipated. If Gary really was that new to the scene, he'd stumbled on quite a find. Both of them had, thought Kieran.

'Where are we off to then? Earl's Court?'

'That sort of thing. Can you just hang on a moment. I shan't be long.'

'Sure,' said Kieran: he'd still some beer left in any case. Gary stuffed *The Swimming-Pool Library* into his shoulder-bag and scurried off with it. He returned almost at once: he must, Kieran thought, have been checking his appearance with the mirror or buying condoms from the machine, because he hadn't had time to do much else.

'Right,' said Gary, 'shall we go?'

Kieran would quite happily have stayed: from the third drink onwards, The Pit always began to seem like home. The bar was filling now; they had to push through the crowd and through a wall of the noise which belonged only in places like this, the eternal turning present of gay disco music:

> It's not the way you lead me by the hand into
> the bedroom,
> It's not the way you throw your clothes upon
> the bathroom floor...

Just before they reached the door, they collided with a moustached middle-aged man and the stripey doughnut.

'Martin,' said Kieran. 'Hello dear.'

'Kieran, how are you?' They exchanged a perfunctory kiss. 'You remember Jason.'

'Yes, vividly. It's a surprise to see you two here.'

'Is it? Well, I do try to keep some tentative hold on reality. If that's what this is. We must meet for a drink sometime.'

'Yes, sure. This is Gary, by the way. We're just off to the rough end of town.'

> It's not the way that you caress me, toy with
>   my affection,
> It's not my sense of emptiness you fill with
>   your desire...

'Well take care. *He* looks as if he could take care of himself, anyway.' Martin gave Gary a long approving glance. Jason meanwhile had mysteriously vanished into the crowd.

'As long as he can take care of me too. Anyway, we'll see you around. Come on.' Feeling proprietorial and pleased with himself, Kieran steered Gary from the bar.

'Wasn't that...?'

'Yes, ridiculous old queen that he is. Still, we'll be all right when he's Home Secretary. Anyway, it was lucky you were there to rescue me.' He squeezed Gary's hand. 'Thank you, dear. Now, Leicester Square tube?'

'Fine.'

They navigated the thinning crowd round the tables outside and an assortment of extremely drunk beggars who seemed to have sprung up with the dusk like mushrooms. At one table a group of boys whom Kieran knew by name looked in their direction and leered stupidly: 'Oh yeah?' said one, replying to the unspoken. 'Coleherne then is it?' A slight breeze was idly re-arranging the rubbish on the pavement. In St Martin's Lane the pre-theatre crowd had been replaced by the more characteristic urban pageant: office-workers afraid to go home, blistered down-and-outs, oriental raiding-parties from Soho, prostitutes, rent-boys.

They had walked only a hundred yards or so when a red car pulled out from a side-street so slender as to be almost invisible and stopped at the kerb beside them.

'We're in luck,' said Gary. 'A lift.'

'Are you sure?'

'Positive.' He opened the rear door. 'In you get.'

'I don't think I've ever been kidnapped before.'

'Well,' said Gary, getting in beside him and slamming the door shut, 'you have now.'

Kieran felt he knew what was happening just before it happened, yet too late all the same. Gary took from his pocket an official-looking ID card and waved it in front of Kieran: he couldn't see the details, but he didn't need to.

'Sergeant Andrew Symes,' said Gary.

'Have I been nicked or something?'

'No, taken in for questioning. Now just think about something else until we get there. And keep your fucking hands off me.'

It ought to have felt like a nightmare, but it didn't. For one thing, Kieran quite often found fear to be at least as exciting as it was frightening. For another, he was sitting next to an extremely pretty young hunk, in the back of a fast car speeding recklessly through the streets of London, which was a desirable circumstance in itself. As usual, when he needed to neutralise his mind, he replayed a symphony in his head - the Shostakovich eighth to which Bertram had taken such an irrational dislike. They were some way west of Kensington, and into the second movement, when the journey ended.

And then the quality of nightmare, or at least of the most profound and unnerving unfamiliarity, did begin to take over. The car turned off into a sequence of side-streets, each narrower than the last, of which the final one terminated in a barrier like that at the entrance to a car-park. The driver offered a plastic card to the machine, and the barrier obligingly lifted. The downward ramp which followed seemed improbably long and was entirely unlit: Kieran thought he could hear through its walls the rumble of a nearby tube-train. Eventually it disgorged them into a high-ceilinged space which might once have been an underground loading-bay. There was a huge rusted lift with a faded sign which said 'Goods Only', and overhead among the girders were metal lamps with oversized but very feeble clear glass bulbs. Kieran remembered that there had been lamps like that in the old gym at school, the place he had hated and feared most, before they demolished it and built a smart new sports hall. More than anything else so far in the evening, the lamps made him afraid.

The car had stopped. 'Right, get out, and don't try to run away. There isn't anywhere you can run to.'

'Where are we?'

'A warehouse in Hammersmith. Where else?'

They walked not to the 'Goods Only' lift but to a heavy ribbed metal door. Again the driver opened it with a card. On the other side was a deserted white-tiled corridor; somewhere, distant but resonant in the harsh acoustic, someone was laboriously typing. Beneath and beyond that, there was a low unsteady hum such as might come from a terminally ill air-conditioning system. Kieran was aware of a faint smell in the air, not unlike that which clung to the staircase at The Pit. Perhaps, he thought, all underworlds are much the same: perhaps this is really the entrance to some especially fetishistic gay bar. 'Pig-warren,' he said reassuringly to himself, and then, parenthetically, '(rabbit-sty).'

Aloud he asked, 'Is there a lavatory? It's the beer,' he added unnecessarily.

Andy gestured at a half-open door. 'In there.'

It was a large, antiquated affair, evidently the subterranean Gents from the building's distant past; for some reason known only to its long-deceased manufacturer, the urinal bore the absurd word 'Radio'. Turning from it after a long luxurious pee, Kieran inspected himself in the pock-marked mirror above the basin. He looked in reasonably good shape, but he instinctively took a comb from the back pocket of his jeans to tidy his hair before noticing that Andy had reappeared in the doorway.

'There's no need for that. Come on.' They walked some way down the corridor. 'Wait in there,' said Andy, opening a door. 'I'll get your file.' He disappeared through a second door. Unable to achieve complete invisibility, the

107

driver wedged himself in a corner and avoided Kieran's eye.

'Cigarette?' asked Kieran, taking a packet from his shirt pocket and lighting one himself. The driver shrugged and shook his head.

The room was small, partly tiled, partly painted dark blue, presumably to discourage graffiti-writers. It was lit by a bare bulb and contained no furniture except a small table, three stacked plastic chairs, and a slatted wooden bench. Someone using a knife had attempted to carve an inscription on the tiled surface. 'Abandon hope,' it began, but the writer had got no further.

It took a long time, or a short cigarette, before Andy returned; Kieran had in fact been smoking with childish urgency, and he was grinding out a long red-hot stub as Andy came through the door. He had taken off his leather jacket and was carrying a thick buff folder and a camera. Through the doorway behind him Kieran could see a small dimly-lit anteroom with a filing cabinet and, beyond that, a more brightly-illuminated but terminably shabby office.

'Right,' said Andy, unstacking the chairs. 'Let's get this over with. It needn't take long. Have a seat.' He flung down the folder on the table and took out a sheet of paper. 'Just glance over the personal details and tell me if they're correct. It saves a lot of questions and answers.'

Kieran glanced. They were not merely correct, they were almost mystifyingly comprehensive, like the biography of someone he'd forgotten he ever knew. There were all the schools from which he'd been expelled, the exams he'd failed, the addresses from which he'd fled with the rent unpaid. There were a couple of silly criminal near-misses - one indecency, the other a daft attempt to get some dope through customs, and it hadn't even been for him. Neither had led to a prosecution, though the second meant that he did tend to be strip-searched at airports. It would probably happen here too.

'You're well-informed,' he said as drily as he could.

'We try.' Andy gave him a short smug smile. 'What we need is a bit more information about your friends, your

signature on a statement, and one or two other boring
formalities, and that'll be it. Let's start with the friends.'

'My friends are simply my friends, and that's it really.'

'You don't deny that you've got political connections?'

'Political? I don't even vote.'

'But you do know Martin Baxter MP, for instance?'

'Do I?'

'You greeted him like an old friend earlier this evening.'

'In that case presumably I do, or did.'

'So that would have been some time ago?'

'What would?'

'When you knew him - like an old friend?'

'Probably. I really don't remember.'

'Let's say four or five years ago.'

'Maybe.'

'At which time you'd have been nineteen or twenty or
thereabouts.'

'Does it matter?'

'It could matter to him. And to us. Where and when did
you meet him?'

'I don't remember.'

Andy leaned towards him - there was the garlic memory
of a takeaway on his breath - and spoke very softly and
slowly. 'Don't be a complete prat, Kieran. You've heard
the stories. Now, where and when did you meet Martin
Baxter?'

'I honestly don't remember.'

'Okay.' Andy seemed to overcome an urge to hit him.
'We'll deal with the boring formality stuff while you try
and remember. Get undressed.'

'What?'

'You heard. I'd have thought that with your track-record
you'd be used to strip-searches. Plus which, I'm going to
need a few photographs for the records, just to make sure
that you match the Kieran Radford in the files in every
particular. Of course, we'll rip your clothes off if you'd get
a kick out of that, but then you'd look bloody silly when
we let you out of here. In fact you might get arrested.' He
turned to the driver. 'I quite like the idea of some

109

uniformed noddy like Greg running him in to the nick for indecent exposure.'

Kieran too glanced at the driver, whose expressionless face seemed to be on the brink of breaking into a sardonic grin. He was surprised to discover how little fear he felt: the sense of nightmare had receded again, to be replaced by the recognition that all this was a weirdly distorted image, like that in a fairground mirror, of things that had happened elsewhere, before. He decided to brazen it out. 'Oh well,' he said, unbuttoning his shirt, an old but expensive salmon-pink one which he suddenly recalled might even have been a gift from Martin, 'just another photo-session.' He had absolutely no doubt that Andy's copious file contained an archive copy of *Vulcan*.

He undressed quickly, piling his clothes on the bench: there was something of the school gym about that, too. 'I usually charge for this,' he said over his shoulder to Andy, who had disappeared into the ante-room.

'We're the ones who do the charging round here.' Andy was pulling on a pair of rubber gloves as he returned. 'Right, turn round.' Facing the tiled wall, Kieran found himself staring at the scratched word 'Abandon' while Andy's gloved hands cursorily searched under his arms, between his legs. 'Okay, face me again.' He saw that meanwhile the driver was examining, with mild distaste, the contents of his pockets. 'Stay there.' Andy stepped back and picked up the camera. 'Look at me.' He snapped away happily. 'Now right a bit.' He seemed to have finished, then he stepped back a couple of paces more, until his back was against the opposite wall, and snapped again. 'Right, that's that. Now take a seat again.'

'Do I get dressed first?'

'No, you sign a fucking statement first. Anyway, it's a warm night.'

'But I haven't made a statement.'

'Yes you have. It's here. Just in case you couldn't remember your affair with Martin Baxter, I decided to compile a summary of our own research. Of course, I'd rather have it in your own words - it would be more authentic - but otherwise this'll have to do.'

Kieran looked at the statement. It seemed simultaneously correct and unrecognisable, somehow reducing him to little more than a powerful man's plaything. It hadn't been like that.

'He didn't give me money.'

'Okay, not money. Presents maybe. Clothes, a watch, a lighter, a monogrammed cock-ring - whatever queers give each other. Presents, right?'

'I suppose so. I don't see why I'm that important.'

'Look, sunshine.' Andy was close-up, quiet and slow again. 'You're not important. You're shit. And shit's disposable, in fact if you don't dispose of it it stinks. You're as important as a photo and a signature which will help us to nail this pillock Baxter. And that's it. So let's have the signature, as it is on your cheque card if you don't mind, so's it's verifiable.'

'Or else?'

'Or else.'

'Right.'

Andy handed him a pen. He pressed it to the paper and willed himself to sign, but some internal physical resistance prevented him. The feeling wasn't unfamiliar: he'd experienced it before when required to sign a form or a cheque under particularly daunting circumstances, and previously he'd forced himself through it. This time, he couldn't. He wanted to tear the statement to bits: whatever world it belonged to, it wasn't his one. He felt a vast baffled anger, but it surfaced only as his obstinate inability to move a pen across the paper.

'I can't do it.'

'Don't make me impatient,' said Andy with care, as if it were a line he'd had to learn.

After what seemed a long, locked moment, the driver materialised behind Kieran and grabbed him by the shoulders. He found himself pulled to his feet, his arms pinned behind him, the driver breathing down his neck. It was a deft move, a piece of teamwork that these two had obviously rehearsed many times. Andy was facing him

111

with an attempt at a sardonic grin.

'Look, Kieran, you're not *worth* hurting,' he said. 'At least, not much.' The first punch got him at the base of the stomach. He felt he was going to vomit, tried to double up, but the driver held him upright. The second and third punches hit him in the balls, the fourth again in the stomach. He choked and retched emptily, suddenly realising that he hadn't really eaten today. Now Andy had him by the hair, raising his head to force eye-contact. 'We've got all night to play with you if we have to,' he said, 'but I expect you'd rather sign now and go home.' Kieran nodded. 'Okay, Trev, plonk him back in the chair.'

'Right.' It was the first time Andy had addressed the driver by name, and the first word the driver had uttered since they'd arrived.

'Now let's get it right this time. Otherwise we'll have you on that bench and do some serious damage. Take your time. Remember it's got to be a proper signature.' Andy handed him the pen.

Kieran realised that his hand was shaking - not trembling exactly, but quivering with a rapid, involuntary vibration. Nevertheless, he was telling himself, the signature was his only way out of here. He had to grip the table hard with his left hand to steady himself while he laboriously wrote it.

'Cheque card?'

The driver picked up the card from the heap on the bench and passed it to Andy.

'It'll do, luckily for you. You wouldn't have wanted a proper session, would you?' He slapped Kieran on the shoulder almost matily, and laughed when Kieran winced. 'Get dressed, and we'll take you home.'

As he did so, he realised that Andy, busy once more with his paperwork, had completely lost interest in him. This, he thought, must be one of the terrible things about rape: it's not so much the humiliation and the pain - that can come with so many kinds of sexual encounter - it's the instant rejection, the sudden reduction to non-existence. Now, disregarded, he felt oddly excluded and isolated, the

112

lonely child in the playground, the coward in the corner of the gym.

'Now,' said Andy, 'you'll go home and you won't make contact with anyone else tonight. Your telephone's disconnected anyway. Tomorrow, if you've got any sense, you'll make arrangements to be well out of London or, better still, England by the weekend. We won't stop you. Your role in this little drama is over.'

'Why should I clear out then?'

'I don't have to tell you this. In fact, I'm not telling you this. Look at this statement you've just signed: have you noticed how the juicy bits with names and dates come at the end, close to the signature? Now you've surely seen leaked documents in the Sunday papers - you know, that ripped-round-the-edges look they give them? This'll do fine. In fact the sole purpose of this statement is for it to turn into a leaked document. And of course we've got some photographs. I was cursing myself for having missed a trick earlier this evening: if I'd had a photographer at that bar I might have got one of you and Baxter kissing. They'd have loved that. Still, the snaps we've got and your statement will give the press what they need. It won't do Baxter's career much good, I'm afraid. And it won't do *you* much good if you're somewhere where Baxter's lawyers can catch up with you - not to mention that tough little bodyguard of his and the rest of the press.'

'Did you say "bodyguard"? What bodyguard?'

'You really don't know? Jason Littlewood. Baxter pays him quite a nice salary: calls him his "research assistant" and even tries to claim him as an expense, I'm told. I'd have thought you'd have known that. What you wouldn't have known is that Jason worked for us for a while: he set up some useful leads, but he got a bit too keen on the research side of things in one way and another. So he won't be too thrilled to find that we've nobbled his lord and master - or is it the other way round? - and that our star informant is none other than an ex-rival and ex-lover. I'd get out if I were you. You've got enough in your bank account.'

'How do you know that?'

'I had it checked out this evening, while we were having our little drink. Do you want to see the balance?'

Andy took a cash-machine printout from the file: it bore the date and time of two hours earlier that evening. Kieran looked at it with a mixture of astonishment and gratitude: Bertram's cheque, which he had wisely paid in at the same branch, had already been credited.

'Where did you get this?'

'Oh, that's easy.' Andy laughed. 'I had a duplicate cash card done for you last week, and we get the PIN numbers from an agency. There's not much that hasn't been hacked into. In fact, there aren't any secrets any more. Life has got rather like pornography, really.' He tossed the spare card in Kieran's direction. 'You may as well have this. Otherwise I might rob you.'

'There's one thing I don't understand,' said Kieran. There were in fact several, but he needed to get to the lavatory again before long. 'If you knew almost everything about me, why tail me on the march, and why hang around to pick me up in a bar?'

'Circumstantial evidence. Getting a feel of the thing. And of course keeping an eye on your friends. At heart I'm just an old-fashioned copper. Now piss off.' He turned to the driver. 'Let him have a wash and then take him home.'

There seemed to be no necessary or possible response to so uncompromising a dismissal. The driver led him out into the silent, deserted corridor - the incompetent typing had ceased, and the low hum had either diminished or merged into the hum inside his head - and flung open the door of the lavatory. Suddenly he was unsteady and acutely aware of an intermittent thudding pain in his guts and in his groin. Standing before the 'Radio' urinal he tried helplessly to vomit and then, steadying himself with one hand on the wall, managed a sore, disjointed pee. That was in every sense a relief, though as he stood there he was uncomfortably aware of the driver's interested gaze on his back. He couldn't for a moment decide whether it was a sexual interest - in which case he didn't stand a chance - or merely a custodial one. He decided on the latter. It was like that odd little ritual in exams at school when, if you needed to go to the lavatory, you had to be accompanied by an invigilator, as if you might have brilliantly concealed all the answers somewhere about the plumbing. Strange how this place kept on flashing up images of school.

Kieran washed his hands, threw some water at his face, caught sight of himself once more in the pock-marked mirror. He looked terrible. Usually when he looked this bad, he was too drunk to care, but now he was horribly, painfully sober. It wasn't even late. Nevertheless, home was where he'd better be, like the man said. Man? He was certainly no older than Kieran, and what was happening in a world in which even the secret policemen seemed young? He thought about the file they had on him, the way it reduced his life to a heap of inconsequential kaleidoscopic fragments: had anyone else noticed that 'file' was an anagram of 'life'? Probably everyone else had. Had the driver? He decided not to ask. He dried his hands on a grey roller-towel and turned, a bit groggily, to the driver. 'Right then, let's go.'

* * *

Clive had worked all day with a kind of contained mania: work, he knew, could be cleansing and refreshing, a strange pure charm against anxiety, and he was determined that it should be so now. All morning he copy-edited *The Radical Urge*, effortlessly refining pomposity and jargon into almost-elegant prose. Usually he liked silence to surround his daytime desk, but today he put on some of Hogwood's Mozart symphonies, as chaste and unprecious as his mood. In the afternoon, he sparkled his way through an editorial conference at his publishers, throwing out bright ideas with the generosity of one who doesn't necessarily expect to put them into practice. They landed around him like luminous grenades, forming small craters among the group of surprised self-serving yuppies whom Bygrave Books these days chose to employ as in-house staff. Then he was due at Colin's for a few drinks and something, if he was lucky, to eat. He had deliberately and guiltily misrepresented this occasion to Kieran as a businesslike meal, in order to exclude him: partly because he did have clear, important things to discuss with Colin, and Kieran's presence always dramatically increased his consumption of alcohol; and partly because Colin and Kieran habitually flirted in a way which Clive had begun to find wearisome.

Colin lived in a flat above a shop in an unfashionable backwater of South London: the walk to it from the tube presented in many ways a mirror-image of Clive's equally unfashionable corner of North London. There was the same sudden impression of litter and decay, the same time-warp transition to parked cars ten years older than those preening themselves at West End meters, the same sour breath of last night's violence in the air. For a while the shop had been a dry cleaners, and Colin had fondly imagined himself to be undergoing a slow poisonous death from noxious chemicals seeping up through the floor-boards. Then it had become a Greek takeaway, owned by a fat semi-kebabed Cypriot who at appointed times during the week would flush away accumulations of grease and blood, so releasing unimaginably nauseous fumes from every drain in the vicinity: the simultaneous visitation of the public health inspector and of a plague of rats had got rid of him. Now it sold prams and children's clothes, and its only recurrent nuisance came from loud babies in parked prams beneath Colin's living-room window.

Only as he pressed the bell at the side-entrance - for Colin was pleasingly oblivious to such modern sophistica-tions as entryphones - did Clive wonder who, if anyone, else might be there. 'Drop round for a drink and a chat on Tuesday' was all he'd said, and there was no telling how many other times he'd said it: Colin had the mysterious ability, or disability, of attracting random discursive people

116

to his presence, which was odd in someone who usually gave the impression of preferring his own and his books' company to anything else. Perhaps it was that which made people regard his friendship as a particular privilege. As he opened the door he, as always, appeared to Clive slightly smaller and slightly balder than when they had last met. He had been a tiny man to start with and was now almost entirely hairless apart from a startling wiry beard of the Brillo-pad variety.

'Hi,' he said breathlessly. His greetings usually had the hurried air of someone caught in the middle of making an omelette. 'Come on up. There's one or two people, but we *will* have a word about that article. Promise.' The one or two people turned out to be a young PE teacher (the latest in a long line) from the school where Colin was Head of History, a detached don from Cambridge who very literally looked down his nose at Clive, a wispy and unsteady Scottish painter, and a huge cumbersome youth who was stretched out sleepily on the sofa, alternately swigging lager from a can and rolling a cigarette.

'Who on earth's he?' Clive whispered to Colin, but the Scottish painter, who had not heard the question, immediately tottered across the room and answered it.

'Clive Greenslade,' he declaimed. 'You're a fine man, a fine editor, aye. Have ye met Tommy? He's a lovely boy, but he's very very shy, is Tommy. Aren't ye, Tommy?' Tommy looked as if he might snarl. 'Aye, but he loves me, does Tommy.'

'Good, wonderful, I'm glad to hear it, Archie,' said Clive, and made for the wine, which was guarded by the Cambridge don.

'Ah yes,' said the don, as if looking up from a Beta-minus essay, 'the *Pendulum* man, isn't it?'

'Yes and no. That would mean I'm well hung and I swing both ways,' said Clive, but the don either didn't hear or didn't understand.

'An interesting little journal. You might care to cast an eye over some work I've been doing on homosexuality in the Imperial Russian Court.'

'That would be fascinating,' said Clive.

It was going to get worse, and it did. The doorbell announced the arrival of an extremely pretty concert pianist who had brought with him a sour, dark acne-pitted youth - apparently a lift-boy from a West End hotel - to whom Tommy seemed to take an immediate, visible and potentially homicidal dislike. Archie, making an extravagant gesture while leaning on the window-sill, dropped a glass onto the exact area of pavement occupied two hours earlier by a particularly raucous infant and seemed soon likely to drop himself there too. In retreat from all this, in pursuit of something to eat, Clive wandered into the kitchen where, as he'd anticipated, there was a table laden with cold food for the taking. Slumped over it at one end was Joe, a sort of younger and more manageable Mick Jagger, who was Colin's occasional lodger and occasional lover, an occasional musician and occasional decorator, whose only full-time occupation during the summer months was improving his suntan. It had been a good summer, and Joe was so superhumanly brown in his skimpy white vest that Clive had to overcome a very powerful urge to discover straight away where, if anywhere, the tan stopped. In fact, in a moment of tiresome omniscience, Clive saw precisely how the evening would turn out. Tommy and the lift-boy would fight. The pianist would go off with the PE teacher. Archie would get more drunk and leave disastrously by door or by window, by taxi or by ambulance. Clive would chat up Joe, only to be interrupted at a crucial point by Colin, who would be quietly upset. Only the dull pedantic Cambridge academic with the fetish about the Imperial Russian Court would remain lord of all he surveyed. It had better not happen. Meanwhile, here was Joe, moping presumably because of Colin's hopeless hobby of collecting PE teachers.

'Hello Joe,' said Clive uselessly. 'How's things?'

'Fucking wankers,' said Joe.

'Yes, I suppose so.' That seemed fairly undeniable. 'Can I steal some food while the others are busy boring each other to tears?'

118

'Help yourself.'

'Thanks.' He helped himself, to salad and cheese and pickles and a slice of extremely good-looking homemade quiche. 'This looks marvellous.' He tasted it. 'It is.'

'I made it,' said Joe, wearily. Clive had forgotten that he was also an occasional chef.

'How's the band?' Clive asked between mouthfuls. Joe played bass guitar with a pop group which had been called alternately Better Dead Than Alive and Half Man Half Meat-Cleaver.

'Split.'

'I'm sorry.' It sounded absurdly funereal. He felt genuinely and simply sorry for poor sad monosyllabic Joe, and put a comforting arm round his shoulders. Though Clive didn't altogether approve of these narcissistic vests, he had to admit that they had certain attractions when the wearer was in need of reassurance. As if by magic, as if by radar, Colin walked into the kitchen.

'How's it going?' Clive asked, quickly returning his attention to his plate.

'Fine,' said Colin. 'Tommy and the lift-boy are getting on splendidly. Apparently they shared the same probation officer.'

'I might have guessed.'

'Might you? Oh, I see. Anyway, that article you want. I've done it. All it needs is typing up.' Colin wrote everything first in excrutiatingly neat, meticulous longhand. 'You'll be glad to hear that I haven't at all approved of this absurd After London idea. It's ridiculous - a throwback to some vague nineteenth century anti-industrial pastoralism in a twentieth century post-industrial society. And it's immoral. If you encourage millions of discontented city-dwellers to up and go off to the country, you're going to make a rare old mess of the country. To say nothing of the city-dwellers.'

Clive laughed. 'Don't you think you're taking a somewhat over-optimistic view of our influence? We're not the *Sun*, you know.'

'Indeed not,' said Colin sniffily, 'and you can't have that

119

both ways, either.'

'Meaning?'

'You'd presumably say that you can't equate influence with circulation, since the *Sun*, in your view, addresses an audience of morons.'

'Broadly, yes.'

'Well, in that case you can't equate lack of influence with lack of circulation, either. Anyway, you're wrong about the *Sun*, that's the worrying part. A lot of its readers are quite smart in their own loathsome way. The trouble with things like *Pendulum* - which of course is marvellous, which is why I'm sweating my guts out over this article - is that they want to change the world without first engaging with the world they want to change. When are you creative people going to take some notice of what society actually is?'

'When society takes some notice of us?' asked Clive.

'Yeah,' said Joe.

The company in the living-room had mellowed and expanded. Archie had taken it upon himself to admit further guests whose acquaintance with Colin seemed tenuous but whose acquaintance with Archie was intimate and effusive. When Clive emerged in their midst carrying a plate, most of the assembled company made a dash for the kitchen. Tommy had closed his eyes, and the remnants of his last roll-up were burning their way into Colin's sofa.

Clive left around mid-evening. He didn't want to be travelling late and alone, not tonight. It wasn't fear, at least no more than usual, it was the need to get home and more precisely to get to the Clarendon before closing-time. He needed to show them - he needed to show the building itself, the bar-stools and the beer-pumps - that he was still around, that it was business as usual in Cliveville, just in case they'd heard a whisper. Not that he thought it was likely: unspeakable happenings were so commonplace these days that no-one *bothered* to speak of them anymore. All the same, when he got home, he'd better try and phone Kieran again.

The tube was playing its nine o'clock limbo game. It

120

was an odd time of the evening: at nine o'clock you couldn't be sure whether the drunks were really drunk or just mildly deranged, while by eleven or twelve you'd know that the drunks were thoroughly rat-arsed and the deranged madly sober. When, after four of the London Underground's elastic minutes, the train eventually arrived, he found himself seated opposite a vast, manicly knitting Middle Eastern woman. As she knitted, her eyes methodically inspected every male in the carriage, starting at the top and moving steadily and unflinchingly down- wards: she looked as if she were silently passing some terrible judgement on each one. When she got halfway down the man next to him, Clive panicked, looking up and away, anywhere to avoid eye-contact. He read and re-read the dreadful dull advertisements for recruitment agencies and condoms, wondering why there were never any interesting or attractive ads on the tube anymore. He knew: they were the underclass, hungry for jobs and condoms; no-one with any status travelled on the tube now, no-one advertisers hoping to make serious money would want to address. Had it always been like that? Surely Clive remembered a time when the tube had been a truly democratic, egalitarian means of travel? Perhaps he was imagining it; perhaps the world had always been this tainted and tacky. He dared to look ahead of him. The knitting woman transferred her attention to a boy with an Adidas bag standing by the doors. So did Clive.

He'd need to change lines at Earl's Court, and stood up to do so. The boy with the Adidas bag was evidently waiting for the station too. He was physical, muscular, more interesting than good-looking. The doors parted and he turned towards the street exit, while Clive would be heading down to the Piccadilly Line. There were thousands of boys like him in London, yet Clive knew with an unshakable conviction who he was. 'Kevin,' he said.

The boy turned, unrecognising but friendly. 'Hi.' The unmistakable chink of metal on metal came from the bag.

'Give my regards to Julian,' said Clive.

'Sure, sure,' said Kevin, turning away again, without

asking his name.

The Piccadilly Line was its usual debauched self. The Piccadilly Line was the experienced, world-weary, veteran whore of the London Underground: unshockable, unstoppable, it held for Clive a sense of deep security which its shabbier though possibly safer siblings mysteriously lacked. It went to almost all the places you could ever want to go. It was linear London. It taught you that Earl's Court and South Ken and Hyde Park and Leicester Square and Covent Garden were all no more than different glosses, different accents or styles of dress, for the same thing. The Piccadilly Line was a mighty fine line.

More than that, its passengers were recognisably people going somewhere. They were actively in transit. Their boisterous chatter announced the theatres or concerts or restaurants or bars to which they were going or from which they had recently emerged. Brightly decorated carrier-bags proclaimed the provenance of their shopping - or, equally often, their shopping-before-last. They were sexy, and one way or another would use their sexiness, although the distinction between those bound for Leicester Square and those for Covent Garden grew daily more difficult to draw. These days Clive was puzzled and almost appalled by the strident sexuality of the young - two punkish lads across the carriage were all over each other, one's hand well and unashamedly into the other's jeans - which had somehow, when he was their age, seemed so much less intrusive, so much less necessary. The truth, he glumly reflected, was that he hadn't particularly wanted or needed a wild sex life until it was too late. There'd been so much to do, and there was *always* going to be time. Until now. Or until that moment, not so long ago, which he now knew he'd always known would occur, when he woke up to find he was forty and his hair was beginning to thin and the constituency of boys who might conceivably want to have sex with him was diminishing faster than his hair.

All the same, the Piccadilly Line remained mildly reassuring, it was still a known territory whose dialects

122

Clive at least slightly understood. There was always at King's Cross the abrupt exit of those real travellers who were heading off north, breakfasting tomorrow in Edinburgh, whom he envied and would one day join. At King's Cross he'd always feel the urge to do it *now*, to get up and go as far as the nearest InterCity would take him. It wasn't much comfort to reflect that these intrepid explorers were more likely late commuters trudging back to homes in absurd places like Baldock and Royston. From King's Cross on the Piccadilly Line changed its argot again. Uh huh, it said, now we're back to the locals, the North London villagers.

And when, almost at the end of the line, Clive stepped off the train and out of the station into his London village, he enjoyed the brief delusion of being home. As he turned into Salisbury Road, he was dimly aware of something different, missing. It took him a moment to register that the proliferating rubbish-sacks on the pavement had been collected and, sure enough, a couple of new sacks, casually flapping in the breeze, were stuffed into the letterbox of his house. He removed them, conscientiously leaving one in the hall for Cath on her return from holiday, and went upstairs. He switched on lamps, drew curtains. He used the lavatory, washed his hands, combed his hair. He tried phoning Kieran, but the number didn't even ring. It was almost ten-thirty.

He found the Clarendon more crowded than he'd anticipated, though he suspected this might be another delusion: any bar tended to seem packed in the last half hour of the evening, not just because the last-minute mob had arrived, but because the other drinkers had relaxed and subsided, taking up more space. Gwylim was behind the bar.

'A pint of our finest?' he asked, pulling it without waiting for a reply. 'I presume Kieran has been seduced back by the bright lights.' Clive realised that he hadn't seen Gwylim since Saturday: for a brightly-coloured landlord, he had a remarkable gift of invisibility.

'Yes, like a moth to a candle-flame, poor dear,' said

123

Clive.

'Some bloody moth,' said Gwylim.

'Some bloody candle,' muttered Clive, but Gwylim had drifted away.

Clive turned to find that Alex had materialised at the bar beside him. It was always a mild shock, this transformation in jeans and sweatshirt, the wrong side of the bar, on his night off.

'You okay?' asked Alex.

'Yes, fine. A long busy day. It's good to be home.'

'No trouble last night?'

'None to speak of. Why?'

'You know. They left a bit sharpish after you, that's all. It looked as if....'

'Did it? So you just stood there, instead of sending out the troops to rescue me? A right knight in shining fucking armour you are.'

'I was on me own here.' Alex looked genuinely pained. 'I did go round Salisbury Road after time. There was only a top-floor light on in your place. No sign of trouble. So I assumed you were okay.'

'I'm sorry.' It was Clive's turn to look pained. 'I didn't mean that, and anyway it would have been mayhem if there'd been other people piling in. It was nothing to get too worried about.' He remembered the title of a song which had meant a lot to him. He grinned. 'I'm still standing.'

'Good. That's good. Tell me about it sometime.'

'Yes, I shall. Sometime. But how about you?'

'What?'

'Everything okay?'

'Yes. I suppose. Work's incredibly boring.' Alex had a daytime desk-job with a building society. 'I actually look forward to being behind the bar here.'

'I can understand that. I used to enjoy it too.' Alex looked mildly surprised. 'Not here, of course. It was the year after university, when I was trying terribly hard to avoid being a teacher - a small hotel bar in the Midlands, but basically quite pubby. It *is* a bit like teaching, actually:

124

keeping the unruly ones in order, keeping the bored ones awake, knowing when to be assertive and when to be invisible. I liked it.'

'You'd probably not like it so much now. It's got a lot rougher.'

'What, here?' Clive looked round the full but unthreatening bar which resembled, in the gaps between Gwylim's sixties tapes, a sound effects track for pub background noise.

'Even here, sometimes,' said Alex.

'Okay, point taken. A drink?' On cue, Dylan appeared beside them. 'Guinness, Dylan?'

'No thanks, mate, I'm just off up the road.' He had with him a pack of canned lager, a distant-looking girl, and the satisfied look of someone who has just discovered a plentiful supply of excellent dope. 'Spliffhead,' said Dylan, explaining the girl. He didn't believe in letting intellectual life get in the way of pleasure.

'Treating the staff?' said Gwylim. He raised a theatrically ironic eyebrow. 'How low can you get?' It wasn't entirely clear which of them he was addressing.

'Why,' Clive asked Alex, 'do you stay here?'

'Which? Here the pub, or the place, or the job, or what?'

'The place and the job, I suppose. I'm so rootless myself, I'm always intrigued by people who manage to stick around where they grew up. I may even be envious, but I'm not admitting it.'

'Can't afford anything else. And mum does me washing, cooks meals when I'm there. When I go, it'll be dramatic.'

'Good, I'll drink to that.'

'Of course, Dylan...,' Alex began, as if reading Clive's thoughts. 'When he was at school, he was an absolute dosser. He got lousy O levels. Whereas I worked like a maniac and did brilliantly. Now look at us. Not fair, really, is it?'

'Or fair in a topsy-turvy way, perhaps. I've been wondering how on earth he got to be called Dylan. Dylan Thomas? Bob Dylan? Is it his real name?'

'No, his name's John. It's Dylan in *The Magic Round-about*, isn't it? You know, the stoned rabbit with the guitar. I'd have thought someone of your age would have got that straight away.'

'You're right, I should have done. When I was at university there was a *Magic Roundabout* Appreciation Society. At least we knew to what extent we were being ironic. These days they watch *Neighbours*, and I bet they use that old excuse about it being so bad it's funny, when in fact they're hooked all along.'

'They just want to wank over Kristian Schmid, that's all.'

'Really?' Clive glanced quickly round the bar. 'That was a bit, well, outspoken for you.'

'Yes, well, I'm off duty, and it's almost closing-time.'

'Anyway, I thought it was the other one - Ryan something.'

'You see!' Alex looked triumphant. 'Even you watch it.'

'No, it was just something Kieran said. Actually that's true. I've never seen the thing. Maybe I'd better start, so that I can at least get my hypocrisy right.'

'I don't think you're missing anything you can't live without.' For a podge he managed a winsome grin.

'Good,' said Clive. He looked at the preposterous grandmaternal clock with which Gwylim had adorned the bar. 'Boing. Time for bed.'

'*What?*'

'*Magic Roundabout*, remember?'

'Oh yes, of course. Well, if you're off, I'll come along with you. Keep you out of trouble in dark alleys.'

'Or even light ones.'

'Come on then. Cheers, Gwylim, see you tomorrow.'

Gwylim waved in an abstracted, about-to-cash-up kind of way. 'I wish you wouldn't call him that,' Clive muttered.

'Whyever not?'

'Well, it was my name for him. That, and Gwyneth. Doesn't he mind?'

'He's got used to it. Lots of people do it now, anyway. It's no worse than John being called Dylan.'

126

Outside there was an odd, unstable peacefulness. There happened, just for that moment, to be not a single moving vehicle in the street, and they crossed easily to the alley which led to Salisbury Road. Somewhere quite near, probably in the churchyard, an owl hooted. It was as if suburbia had gone to sleep. Then, of course, a juggernaut rumbled by, followed by the usual vexed retinue of cars.

They turned out of the alley and into Salisbury Road. A big pink harvest moon wallowed absurdly beyond the houses, beyond the multi-storey car park, like a tethered airship.

'As you're here,' said Clive, 'you might as well be my excuse for finishing off a bottle of scotch. There's probably only a drop left. Fancy some?'

'Yes, cheers.'

'It's probably a bit of a tip,' Clive apologised as they climbed the stairs. 'I've actually been rather busy. No time to do the housework.' But it all looked neat enough: he had, after all, been round the entire flat putting things back in their places after Kieran's weekend visit, as if reassembling the contents of a doll's house. He went into the kitchen and poured two huge whiskies: there was in fact almost half a bottle left. He flung in ice-cubes to disguise the enormity of the drinks and took them into the living-room.

'Bloody hell,' said Alex.

'It's the ice makes it look a lot.'

'Even so.' He was, of course, a barman. 'Cheers.' Clive realised, as Alex glanced round the room, that it was the first time he'd actually been inside the flat. It was always intriguing to watch someone sizing up the space in which you lived, trying to deduce what really caught their admiration or revulsion. And Clive knew that his living-room usually made a decisive impression on other people. It didn't have the flash legacies of eighties materialism - the carpet was cheap and threadbare, the furniture shabby, the sound system ancient apart from the CD player, and he didn't even possess a video - but there were books and discs and pictures, odd pieces of pottery, leafy plants, good

127

lighting. People didn't always know how to take it.

'It's a marvellous room,' said Alex, with uncharacteristic enthusiasm. 'Lots of real things. I like that. Where do you work?'

'Upstairs, in the studio. It's midway between a second floor and a loft conversion, but it gives me good space and a break from all the domestic stuff down here. Wander round if you like.'

Alex wandered. He went up to the studio and switched on the ceiling light.

'Bloody hell, that's a bit harsh.'

'Purposeful, Alex, purposeful. You hardly notice when there's a desk lamp on too.'

'And an even older record player,' said Alex delightedly. 'And a stack of really *old* LPs.' Finzi was still on top, but with unerring instinct Alex dived to the embarrassing bottom of the pile. 'Neil Young. James Taylor. I don't believe this: The Mamas and Papas.'

'Well.' Clive felt genuinely and perplexingly cornered. 'It's the past. We all have one. In the end.' Mercifully, Alex showed no desire to hear The Mamas and Papas. There was quite enough of that on Gwylim's nostalgia tapes at the Clarendon.

'So, what happened?' Alex asked, when they were back in the living-room again.

'Not a lot,' Clive said. 'A few kicks, not a lot.' But with one hand he instinctively nursed his ribs, for a moment resisting the admission which would have gone with nursing his crotch as well.

Alex crossed the room to him, smiling. 'Let's have a look at it,' he said briskly, the dressing-room physio. It was a convincing persona, and Clive allowed himself to believe it, despite the smile. He took off his shirt and stretched out as luxuriously as he could manage on the sofa. Alex explored the damaged area with unexpectedly supple fingers. 'It's all right,' he said, grinning. 'I've genuinely done a course in this.'

'Whatever for?'

'Thought it might come in handy at the rugby club. In

128

one way or another.'

'You're good with your hands,' said Clive, meaning it. They both laughed. 'As the actress said to the bishop. Or vice versa.'

'Why did they go for you? A bit organised for queer-bashing, wasn't it?'

'Oh, they'd been tipped off. Someone somewhere doesn't love me. I make noises, only little noises, that don't go down well in some quarters. Ouch.'

'Sorry. So what are they trying to do?'

'Shut me up, I suppose, and scare me out of London.'

'Will you go?'

Clive thought he was going to say no. 'Probably yes,' he said.

'That'll be a pity.'

'Thanks.'

'Anywhere else?'

'Sorry?'

'Did they get you anywhere else?' But Alex, not needing to be told, was already reaching for the zip of Clive's jeans.

'Don't you think,' said Clive carefully, 'that if we're going to undress each other we'd be better off in the bedroom?' They regarded each other steadily for a moment and then Clive, reaching up for Alex's shoulders, gently pulled him down to his own level and kissed him.

'Okay,' said Alex. As they squeezed along the corridor in an awkward embrace, he added with a disconcerting regression into childhood innocence, 'But I mustn't be late.'

✳ ✳ ✳

Andy watched television. He watched sumo wrestling, in which fat men hurled themselves at each other. He watched *Prisoner: Cell Block H*, in which fat women hurled themselves at each other. From both he obtained a sexless catharsis, as if if the participants were too gamily absurd, like rugby balls or balloons, to be objects of desire. He watched late night movies and crappy soaps in which the merest hint of female sexuality was enough to trigger his vague, focusless lust. He watched ads for cars and jeans and after-shave which made him feel competitive or vindictive or both: it was hard to tell the difference.

Andy ate chilled junk food or takeaways from the Indian. His local friendly Pryceryte had an especially noxious line in ravioli which, he was certain, was slowly poisoning him. However carefully he read and followed the instructions on the carton, the stuff still left a bitter chemical aftertaste on the roof of his mouth, where it stayed until its next lager-shampoo. He went back for more. It became addictive, it appealed to his enquiring spirit: he needed to discover whether every single pack had this mystery ingredient and whether he could indefinitely withstand its continued onslaught. The Indian offered altogether more subtle, sophisticated pleasures. Young Pritam - the twenty-year-old genius who ran it, and the newsagents, and the laundrette, and God only knew what else - also dealt, inevitably, intuitively, in drugs. Andy had quietly busted him and could have got him some very special treatment inside from the New Britain boys. He hadn't done that. Instead, he and Wayne and Dean had marched into the kitchen one evening, in front of the thirteen-year-old chefs, and grabbed Pritam. They'd stretched him out on the table and explained the situation to him in terms which left no room for misunderstanding. The Indian kids had stood round in freeze-frame with implements in their hands while Andy had playfully indicated some of the things which a simple kitchen knife, to say nothing of a blender or liquidizer, might do to a prone Pritam. 'Next time, Pritam, next time,' he'd said, and slapped his arse jovially before striding out the door.

So Pritam treated him well, with a ludicrous deference which perked up Andy's failures of days, and if some poor fool had to be set up for a drugs bust Pritam would happily assist. Yet Andy couldn't entirely blind himself to the fact that rather few people treated him well, and those who did either feared him or owed him. He'd been surprised to discover how little Kieran Radford feared him, how emotionally wasted he himself had felt at the end of the evening. He'd got what he needed, certainly, and the pursuit had been enjoyable, even instructive - what he'd said about being an old-fashioned copper wasn't entirely untrue, even if he'd stolen the thought from Greg Thornton - but in the end there'd been no buzz. From the start he'd been outflanked by a kind of streetwise knowingness, a blend of calm and camp, which he couldn't get beyond. For a moment, when he'd handed out those carefully-placed punches, he'd thought there might be some mileage in it, a chance of the man-to-man confrontation he understood. But no, the kid had suddenly turned inert, passive, he dullest kind of victim. He'd switched off everything there was to work against in him. It was as if he'd been taking victim-lessons all his life.

Andy, by contrast, had been taking power-lessons all his life. With the example of the church's benign blathering incompetence constantly before him, he'd constructed his destiny in terms of a flexible, pragmatic fanaticism. His school, a liberal and well-intentioned but altogether rather dim comprehensive, had merely served to confirm his views. There he'd evolved into the archetypal schoolboy rebel, though not quite for the reasons people like Greg supposed. His teachers had wanted him to go to university, had gone out of their way to help and encourage him - his father was the vicar, after all - but he'd had to show that he had the power to thwart their plans. Then, at the height of his post-school wildness, he'd suddenly had his hair cut, smartened himself up, and gone off to Hendon: to him it seemed almost inevitable, like completing a full circle. His rebellious friends were appalled, of course: perhaps they sensed that he now had a new kind of power over them too.

Andy felt perfectly at liberty to vary his fanatical beliefs from day to day - depending on the circumstances or the assignment or the state of his hangover - as long as the beliefs were, at any given moment, clear and uncomplicated. He rather regretted that this current assignment kept dragging him into murky areas where the clear target got fogged out. When it was over, soon tomorrow, the next day, he hoped he'd be onto something bigger, sharper: the IRA, for instance. That would make a change from pathetic little queers like Kieran Radford. Power in action, clearly vindicated, that was all, that was all.

Soon, tomorrow, the next day. He lay back on his narrow bed in the standard-issue room, watched over dispassionately by the women on his wall, and thought about the future. Viewed through the comforting haze of a day-dream, the future could present itself in familiar, unambiguous images: the silver-grey BMW; the executive house with its big walled garden and pool; the best hi-fi and video; Debbie and the kids (kids?) basking in his prosperity. He grudgingly daydreamed Debbie a Metro so that she wouldn't be in danger of wrecking the BMW. He knew of course that there was virtually no chance of him actually marrying Debbie.

But the future was also, and more immediately, tidying up the loose ends of the Baxter business tomorrow, getting down to Southampton afterwards, getting his hands on some worthwhile assignment after that. He needed something big to work on: he needed a break. Somewhere inside - and it was his one deep, naggingly unavoidable worry - he knew that he couldn't go on for very much longer in the police digs with the disgusting junk food, the Indian takeaways, the increasingly sharp reproaches of Greg Thornton. He needed promotion.

SIX

Clive dreamed he was in a theatre - or possibly, since the audience was distributed in steep tiers on three sides of the stage, a vast and unfamiliar concert hall. How he had got here he wasn't sure: swept along by the crowd into a foyer, he'd mysteriously discovered a ticket marked 'Door E' in his hand; no less mysteriously, there were friends of his in the packed foyer - Tim and another actor called Sam, whom he hadn't seen for *years* - and they shouted across to him 'We must have a drink afterwards' before heading in the opposite direction, towards Door B. Looking across the audience, across the front of the stage almost, he'd watched them taking their seats in the packed house. Now the performance was apparently coming to an end: it seemed to have been a one-man show by a pop-star turned actor-entertainer, exactly the sort of thing to which he'd never go, and he hadn't seen or heard a word of it. And now the theatre was emptying: more precisely, it had already emptied entirely except for the stragglers in his own section of the audience.

He eventually pushed his way out through the foyer into the street to find, not much to his surprise, that everyone he knew had vanished. Since he didn't know how he'd arrived here, he had no idea how to get home: the streets were narrow and shabbily domestic - terraced houses, modest shops and darkened pubs - like the backstreets of a semi-derelict provincial town. There were 'For Sale' boards on which the letters had faded almost to illegibility nailed over doorways, sad remnants of curtains flailing helplessly from shattered windows. Suddenly he found himself running to catch up with a girl who'd been, like him, one of the last to leave the theatre and who was now walking briskly away down a side-turning. 'Excuse me,' he said breathlessly, 'is this the way back to the West End?' 'Oh yes,' she replied, 'I expect so.' Unsure of what else to do, and aware only that there was no point in staying where he was, he followed her.

They reached a junction, at which point two other girls appeared from the gloom, the three of them chattering and giggling incomprehensibly. Then from the right-hand turning, a furious hag emerged (Clive had instantly a sense of Hecate and the witches from the interpolated scenes in *Macbeth*), loudly scolding the other three who fled, chortling, down the left-hand turning. He headed after them but they disappeared completely, although he could still hear them, and he was left standing on a craggy coastline, staring out at a dark placid sea. Where was he? The water seemed, though he didn't know why, to be the North Sea in an unusually sociable mood, yet these huge rocks surely didn't belong to the East Anglian coast he knew. So he must be much further north, and far from any city.... Feeling almost rebellious about this absurd sequence of events, he retraced his steps. The Hecate-figure was no longer obstructing the right-hand turning, so he took that. Before long, he was in misty open country, and he could just make out some shapes, like megaliths, at the side of the road. As he got closer, he saw that they were indeed standing stones, disconcertingly gold and amber in colour, and grouped in a loose circle. There was an official-looking sign - the sort which gives you a potted history and warns you not to steal bits of the monument - at the edge of the circle, but it was in some vaguely oriental-looking language which Clive couldn't understand.

He walked on, aware that his foggy country road was becoming vaguely urban again and that he was approaching a T-junction. When he reached it, opposite him there were railings, pillars, gates, a courtyard and an imposing academic building beyond. For a moment he thought it might be a Cambridge college, but a second look told him that it was the British Museum and that he was somehow back in London.

Abruptly awake, Clive gratefully observed the bed's disarray, the satisfyingly bruised look which said it had

134

been used rather than merely occupied. He felt pleasantly used too: a distant aftertaste reminded him that Alex's body, which he had so comprehensively if incomprehensibly explored, had a musky, musty tang to it, not unlike tortilla chips. There was, that summer, so much going wrong around him that for Clive the fact of an unpremeditated occasion going right seemed like a breath of warm autumn, a brilliant reprieve. With close friends like Kieran it was different: you psyched yourself up for intimacy, you were prepared for demands made and met, you knew the limits. With total strangers it was different again, or it had been in the less paranoid past, the brief encounter uncomplicated by history and uninhibited by a future. Alex, of course, had left somewhere in the early hours, too young perhaps to value the pleasures of an all-night embrace and a slow shared awakening, or perhaps simply worried about a worried mother who'd expected him home.

Clive got up, shaved, washed, and fell into the bath for a ruminative half-hour. Kieran had often tried to persuade him to the superior merits of showering, but Clive found it almost impossible to function either mentally or physically until his body had been horizontally immersed in water for a while. In his morning bath he had designed incredible cities, composed great symphonies, written whole novels. He wished that he had also been able to invent a machine which would plug into his bathed brain and convey its thoughts onto paper. This morning, he re-ran his strange dream, and wondered what it meant, or whether dreams meant anything at all.

He breakfasted in the kitchen on orange juice, healthy cereal, wholemeal toast, and glanced over the morning paper. Inflation was marginally down, unemployment substantially up. There were reports of a supermarket food-poisoning scare, a nuclear power-station scare, and a chemical pollution in tap-water scare; on the science page, a medical conference had scarily concluded that all these scares were endangering the nation's psychological health. The Home Secretary had described as 'mischievous, ridiculous, and utterly without foundation' an allegation that a secret police department called RAID was routinely ill-treating suspects in order to obtain information which might be politically beneficial to the government. There was a warning of severe weather: Hurricane Norman was likely to bring strong winds, storms and flooding to the North and West by Sunday.

From the kitchen window, Clive watched the birds in the courtyard garden below, where he had thrown out some stale bread. There was definitely something going wrong this summer. The sparrows were behaving strangely, for one thing. He'd always thought of sparrows as artful and perky but essentially unaggressive birds, yet out there this morning they were actually chasing away the starlings. And the starlings, who normally seemed to approach any food with all the subtlety and single-mindedness of can-openers, were backing off, hobbling sideways, and reproaching each other with sad quacks. Meanwhile, the sparrows, in-between balletic little squabbles amongst themselves, were devouring all the bread with much cheeping and wing-flapping. Perhaps, thought Clive, the reign of sparrows has finally arrived.

He went downstairs to pick up the post. In late August even his mail seemed to take on a malevolent dullness. There was an invitation to review a probably unintelligible book, a few bits and pieces of *Pendulum* business, a word-processor-personalised (No Medical Required!) letter urging him to apply for some insurance policy, and a form apparently filled in by an illiterate schoolgirl addressed to Mr Clive Greenslope from his tax inspector drawing attention to a discrepancy of £86.13 from three years ago about which he had already written seven unanswered letters. There was also, from Jeremy Barnes, a postcard showing the Curlew River window from the Britten memorial triptych in Aldeburgh parish church, hoping that Clive would be able to make it to Suffolk for the weekend. Clive hoped so too.

＊ ＊ ＊

Earl's Court was full of evasively respectable-looking terraced streets calling themselves Gardens, and it took Andy a few moments to remember which one of them also called itself Swinburne. He'd better go and have his little chat with old Philpotts, and then he hoped this silly episode would be over. It would be a long day. Andy worked a patchwork of shifts as and when he was needed: although it meant his spells of duty were often practically overlapping - as yesterday evening and now this morning - it also meant that useful stretches of free time could appear mid-week. This afternoon, he'd drive down to Southampton, take Debbie out for a meal this evening, and with any luck stay the night before heading back to London around crack of dawn, whenever that might be.

Andy drove round to Earl's Court, knowing all the time that it would probably have been quicker to take the tube and walk, and eventually found a parking meter a number of Gardens and Villas away from Swinburne. He took from the glove compartment a yellow sack which said 'OUT OF USE - METROPOLITAN POLICE' and tied it over the meter: since the traffic wardens had been privatised it was best not to take chances, even though it always reminded him of putting a budgerigar to bed. As he got out of the car, he felt not exactly doubt but a sense of the void within himself where doubt might have been: he had to admit that he didn't know quite what to expect. Nevertheless, he set off briskly on foot. For once, Andy was well-dressed: light suit, striped shirt, modestly patterned tie. By the time he reached Bertram's door, he felt less like a secret policeman than a rep: two decorators, apparently sharing this impression, smiled condescendingly down at him from a nearby scaffolding. He studied the labels on the entryphone panel: '1', which was at the bottom, said 'Philpotts'; '2', above it, said 'Col & Mrs Fairhaven'; '3', above that, said simply 'Rick' - another name had been obliterated. He pressed the button for Flat 1 and waited.

137

There was a long pause, and then 'Philpotts!' came an exclamatory voice like that of an intrepid explorer on a short-wave radio.

'Sergeant Symes, sir, police. I wonder if I might have a few words. Just a routine enquiry, sir.'

'Good heavens,' said the entryphone. 'Yes, one moment.'

It was a very long moment, but Andy wasn't surprised when Philpotts came to the door in person, as he lived in the ground-floor flat. He was, however, surprised to find that the old man was bundling an extremely fierce and talkative little Italian woman out of the door in front of him.

'That's Francesca,' said Philpotts as he waved her down the steps. 'My lady who does,' he added confidentially, as if she might be offended by the description.

'Ah, I see, sir,' said Andy, relieved. For a nasty instant he'd wondered whether he was about to make a complete fool of himself. 'My identification, sir.' He waved the plastic-covered card under Philpotts' nose. 'May I come in, sir?'

'Yes, of course, although I don't know.... Yes, this way.'

Philpotts led the way through an entirely featureless hall to the door of his flat. He was dressed in old clothes - shirt and trousers left over from his business days, Andy supposed, and an oatmeal-coloured cardigan - and managed to appear both solid and fragile at the same time.

'Come in,' said Philpotts, opening the living-room door. 'Take a seat.'

'Thank you, sir,' said Andy, choosing the least comfortable chair. 'You've got a lot of books.'

'Yes.' Philpotts sank wearily onto the sofa, as if he hoped to vanish into it completely. 'I suppose I have.'

'I'm sorry, sir. People must always be saying that.'

'No, as a matter of fact they're not. Most of the people who come in here simply take them for granted. But there are, I agree, a great many. However, I can't imagine that you came here to congratulate me on my library.'

You had to admire these old buffers, Andy thought. Philpotts had been rattled, seriously rattled, at first, but already he was nestling into a kind of protective urbanity which, Andy knew, would be impossible to break through once it became established. He'd have to upset him a bit before that happened.

'I'm afraid not, sir. Are you acquainted with a young man called Kieran Radford?'

'Why? Is he in some sort of trouble?'

'Not exactly *in* trouble, sir, though you might say he's had a close encounter with it.' He let a mysterious smile briefly pass over his lips. 'Let's say that he's not the ultimate focus of our enquiries, but that we need to fill in as much background as we can. You do know him, then?'

'Yes, he's a very gifted and intelligent young man, and a most promising writer.'

'And?'

'And that's that.'

'You don't have any more personal involvement, shall we say, with him?'

'My dear young man, if what you're trying to say in your cumbersome way is "Is he a homosexual?", then of course the answer is yes,' said Philpotts, with surprising energy. 'So am I. It isn't an offence, you know, and it isn't any of your business. We're both consenting adults over twenty-one. I should have thought that was rather obvious in my case.'

'Yes, sir, I take that point, of course. I was simply trying to get an accurate picture. But it does bring me to an important question. Mr Radford does appear to be very young, doesn't he?'

'Yes, charmingly so.'

'And how long might you have known him?'

'A couple of years, at most.'

'And where did you meet him?' asked Andy. 'If you'll forgive my saying so, I can't imagine you frequenting bars like The Pit.'

That, he saw at once, was a mistake: Philpotts gave him an arch glance as if to suggest that he was still perfectly capable of frequenting The Pit if he so chose.

'At a party given by a mutual friend.'

'Might I ask which mutual friend?'

'No.' Philpotts managed a slight pout with this.

'It wouldn't by any chance have been a Mr Martin Baxter?'

'It might have been. In fact it quite probably was.'

'Do you know Mr Baxter well?'

'We know each other socially.' Philpotts suddenly looked very bored and exhausted. 'You do have to realise that as a publisher - well, as an ex-publisher - I naturally tend to bump into writers and other public figures. It's not at all surprising. I expect you find yourself going to all sorts of parties full of, well, police people.' Philpotts threw a glance of unmistakably camp surmise at Andy. 'No doubt you like the uniforms.'

'No, sir, as it happens we tend to remain rather aloof from the uniformed lot.'

Philpotts seemed to consider this seriously and to be genuinely disappointed. 'How frightfully dull.'

Andy felt wrong-footed, and didn't quite know why, but there was little he could do except blunder on. 'Now, let me get to the point - or one of them. Would you think it likely, simply as a matter of conjecture, that Kieran Radford had been involved in an intimate relationship with Martin Baxter prior to that meeting?'

Philpotts suddenly hooted a kind of with mirth, as if the penny had dropped in so ticklish a way that he couldn't resist it. 'You mean, what you're really trying to deduce is whether Baxter had an illegal affair with Kieran while Kieran was under twenty-one. Well, if he did, the stains will have been washed out long ago. In any case, I'm buggered if I know. And to be honest, I'm buggered if I care.'

'Thank you, sir, you've been a great help,' said Andy, as coolly as he could. He took two photographs from his jacket pocket. 'Would you say,' he asked, passing the first one to Philpotts, 'that that's a good likeness?'

Philpotts looked at the head and shoulders and the tiled wall, like that of a public lavatory.

'Yes, but...?'

140

'Yesterday evening, at the nick. I'll grant you it doesn't look much like a nick. That's part of the charm. It's one of the photos we might have to let the papers have, if a story breaks. The other one' - Andy passed it across - 'is probably for a more specialised public.'

It was one of the final couple he'd taken, when he'd stepped back to get a full-length shot. He'd sensed it would come in handy.

Philpotts appeared temporarily stunned and then, perhaps as a defence, almost crotchety. 'He even poses in a police station, the little tart. He'll do anything to be photographed.'

Andy laughed. He suddenly, and slightly to his own surprise, felt almost friendly towards Philpotts. 'Well, it is rather a special police station. Keep them as souvenirs. I've got copies.'

Philpotts seemed to search around in bewilderment for some appropriate conventional response. 'Thank you. That's kind, I suppose, in some odd way.' Somewhere in the flat a clock grumbled and chimed. 'I should have offered you some coffee while we were chatting. Would you like some before you go? Or do policemen always drink tea?'

'Coffee would be fine,' Andy said. He didn't particularly want to drink it, but he wouldn't mind a snoop round the living room while Philpotts was busy in the kitchen.

'It'll have to be instant, I'm afraid. The percolator's fucked.'

'No problem,' said Andy, not for the first time marvelling at the way in which easy obscenities slipped into Philpotts' urbane dialect.

At the door Philpotts turned and said, 'I may be a few minutes. I'll take some coffee out to those decorators: there's nobody in next door.' Andy smiled encouragingly: he guessed that the younger one with the tattoos might have some passing interest for Philpotts, and found that he had to re-interpret their ironic downward glances at him as he'd waited outside the front door.

The old man pottered off to the kitchen and noisily filled a kettle. Andy stood up and looked around the room: there had to be something wrong somewhere. there was in every room, something which the occupant had ceased to notice but which gave the game away. The room was disarmingly clean - freshly polished furniture, empty ashtrays - but that was hardly surprising or suspicious since Philpotts' 'lady who does' had only recently done. Otherwise, the place looked and smelled old, like the study of a retired schoolmaster or an elderly clergyman: it wasn't that the things in it were unused, just that each of them knew its way home. There were books everywhere, and those stacked horizontally, as if lately perused, reflected the same odd mix of styles as Philpotts' vocabulary: volumes of memoirs and fat biographies rubbed covers with *Male Photography Omnibus* and *Berliner Jungs*. On the desk there was a small bronze nude used as a paperweight; on the one bookless wall, a bright painting of naked men initialled 'ML'. Andy was used to unearthing guilty secrets: the trouble with Philpotts was that in hiding nothing he seemed to have nothing to hide.

The only flagrant anachronism in this confidently settled place, apart from the CD player which for a music-lover would be a simple necessity, was the video. Andy looked hard at that, and at the bookshelves nearest to it: there were tapes of operas and of Shakespeare plays, and next to them a row of dull boxes with neat scholarly lettering on their spines. He took one of the boxes at random - it was improbably labelled 'Tales of the Farmyard' - and slipped the tape into the machine, taking care to turn down the sound. He heard the flat door open and hoped the decorators would detain Philpotts for another minute or two. Then he stood back and watched.

The scene was a barn of some description, full of hay or straw - Andy had never been sure which was which - and in the middle of it was an ancient pre-war Morris car. Bits of the car were strewn about the barn, as were spanners and other tools, and from beneath the engine a pair of bare legs protruded. Clearly someone was tinkering away under there, and if he wasn't careful he was likely to kick over the can of motor oil which stood near his feet. Then two young labourers, wearing jeans and nothing else, and rather quaintly carrying pitchforks, strode in. They looked at the legs and leered at each other. Without more ado, each grabbed a leg and pulled. A naked well-built lad of about eighteen slid out into the hay, or straw, trying unconvincingly to look shocked and surprised. The camera lingered on him affectionately for a moment before the pitchfork carriers, one of whom had put down his pitchfork and picked up a spanner, yanked him over so that he was face-down: he didn't seem to resist very much, but perhaps he wasn't being paid by the minute. The spanner-carrier held him down while the other peeled off his jeans and jovially picked up the can of Duckham's.

It was fairly easy to guess what would happen next, although in fact Andy didn't see, for at this point Philpotts returned carrying a tray which contained two cups of coffee together with a silver cream jug and sugar bowl. To his credit, and to Andy's surprise, he didn't drop the tray but carefully set it down on a table before glancing again at the television and back to Andy and saying, 'Oh dearie me.'

'I'm sorry,' said Andy, not entirely meaning it. He could use this, somehow. 'I'll have to take that little lot away with me. I'll give you a receipt, of course.'

'Yes, I see. Will this mean...?'

'Not necessarily. I'll have to ask my boss about it. I'll be able to let you know within a day or so. You aren't thinking of leaving the country, are you?'

'Leaving the country?' Philpotts seemed astonished and impressed by the idea. 'No, absolutely not.' The second labourer, now also naked, seemed about to do something unspeakable with the spanner. 'Do you think we might switch that off? I'm beginning to feel a little queasy.'

Andy turned the machine off and removed the tape, at the same time gathering a small stack of them from the bookshelf. Philpotts meanwhile sipped his coffee with a pretence at control which must have been winding him up

143

inside: when Andy left, he'd probably break down completely. Still, that couldn't be helped. Meanwhile, a last chance, slender and ignoble as it was, had to be taken.

'You're quite certain,' said Andy, 'that you can't recall anything specific which might help us with our enquiries about Martin Baxter and Kieran Radford? I mean, that might make things easier with this other business.'

'I can't help you,' said Philpotts firmly. 'In any case, I only ever gossip about the distant past. And then only to friends.'

'Right, I'll write you out a receipt,' said Andy, taking a pad from his jacket pocket, 'and then if you've a carrier-bag of some sort to put these in, I'll be off.'

Philpotts stood up creakily - again Andy had the sense of extreme fragility beneath the controlled surface - and soon returned from the kitchen with a large blue-and-green carrier-bag. On it were the words 'heffers: cambridge'.

'A dear friend of mine who's a don brought me some very fine books in this.' Philpotts managed to giggle. 'I can't quite imagine what he'd say if he saw it being refilled with *those.*'

'I expect he'd say it was all art, sir.' Andy felt rather pleased with this remark but Philpotts didn't respond. 'Thank you for the coffee. I'll find my own way out.'

But Philpotts naturally followed him, pottering all the way to the steps onto the street, presumably to make sure that he really did go, and no doubt watching him as he walked jauntily away down the pavement, swinging the Heffers carrier-bag and feeling extremely pleased with himself. It hadn't worked out as he'd expected. It had worked out better. He didn't need old Philpotts to talk dirty about Martin Baxter - he had enough to start that one moving - but now he'd picked up a nice little supporting act which could put him one jump ahead of anywhere Bob Clarke might imagine him to be. He leapt into his car, almost forgetting to unshroud the sleeping parking-meter, and dashed back to base in his flashiest boy-racer style.

He'd been working on some pornography seizures a few weeks back, so his little basement office, impoverished as it was in most respects, had the temporary luxury of a television and video which he'd of course been meaning to return to the equipment store. He knew he'd better talk to Clarke, as unsmugly as possible, but there was something irresistible about a bag of untried video cassettes. He took one out at random. This one was labelled 'Great Railway Journeys' in the same scholarly style which he now knew to be an arch joke. When the image on the screen sprang into life, he couldn't believe his eyes: a steam-hauled pullman train was drawing out of a London terminus maybe thirty or forty years ago, and on the sound-track some busy string music was almost immediately overlaid with the unmistakable intonation of the Movietone News announcer. 'You bastard,' said Andy aloud to the screen: perhaps that was why Philpotts had giggled about him taking the tapes. But no, Philpotts wasn't that devious, or at least he wasn't devious in quite that way: there was something almost endearingly innocent about him, and it might infuriatingly prove to be the kind of innocence which rejoiced in films of old railway engines. Still, if this one failed him, Andy had the incriminating farmyard tape. Reminding himself that he mustn't underestimate Philpotts' quirky sense of humour, he fast-forwarded; before long, as he'd hoped, there was an abrupt break. He pressed Play again.

A very lanky boy in Lycra shorts with a racing bike was trying to persuade a hunky black British Rail guard to let him stow his bike in the guard's van. The guard finally - in fact quite swiftly - agreed, and the two of them lifted the bike in, wedging the front wheel with apparently unnecessary firmness between a pair of large parcels. The plots of these things, as Andy well knew from their heterosexual counterparts, were usually thin on all motives but one, and next the boy, for no clear reason, bent forward over the saddle as if searching for something which might be attached to the handle-bars. What *were* very soon attached to the handle-bars were the boy's wrists, with some thick parcel-twine the guard happened to have lying around, and very soon after that his shorts were being

145

peeled off, leaving him helplessly bent over the saddle. Andy decided to let them get on with it while he phoned Bob Clarke's secretary.

'Hello, Angela? It's Andy Symes, your man in the basement.' He knew that all the women in the building fancied him to distraction. Apart from that, these videos were making him feel quite horny in an unfocussed way. Angela didn't sound in the same mood, though. Perhaps she needed a video of her own.

'Yes, Andrew, how can I help you?'

'Would it be possible to have a quick word with his lordship?'

'I'll see if Detective Inspector Clarke is available. Hold the line, please.'

There was no cricket on the radio, so he should be, thought Andy. He was.

'Hello, Clarke speaking.'

'Hello, sir, it's Andrew Symes. I thought you might like to know of a new angle on the Martin Baxter business.'

'A *new* angle? Well, I've only got the Radford statement and photographs on my desk this morning. Good work, by the way. Just what the *Sunday Herald* wants. It was a neat trick to get him photographed in a public lavatory. I won't ask where the lavatory was.'

'That wasn't a lavatory, sir. That was our interview room down here.'

'Was it? Bloody hell. Anyway, what's this new angle?'

'I went and had a chat with Bertram Philpotts this morning - he's the retired publisher who's a friend of Radford and Baxter. I got nothing worth having on Baxter.'

'But?'

'But I did walk out with a bagful of pornographic gay videos.'

'Well, that's very ingenious, but I don't really see how it helps us.'

'It doesn't directly. It's just that I thought if we charge him, we've got a supporting act. The tabloids can have the Baxter rent boy scandal, the heavies can have "Publisher on Porn Video Charge". It won't take long for some genius

146

to lock the stories together, and there you are - Baxter linked to a porn video racket as well.'

'That does sound quite useful. Well done. Get the details up to me by lunchtime and I'll give you the go-ahead by tomorrow morning if it all adds up. I'll have to make one or two calls just to check that we're not treading on sensitive toes by charging Philpotts. You're on tomorrow morning, are you?'

'Yes.'

'Good. Get the details up to me, then.'

Andy felt that, considering how bright - apart from how just plain lucky - the move had been, he'd managed to contain the smugness. He turned back, with little more than cursory interest, to the television screen. The scene had changed again. This time it was a compartment inside a moving train, the sort without a corridor that were probably still trundling around on the remoter bits of the old Southern Region. Illogically, a ticket-collector stood with his back against the door, as if he'd just walked in from the non-existent corridor: it was the same big black guy, though looking a bit younger, as the guard in the previous sequence, and he was wearing the tightest-fitting BR uniform Andy had ever seen. He checked the tickets of two commuters sitting opposite each other by the door, the advanced to the camera's corner to check the camera's ticket - while the camera, of course, admired his crotch. When he turned to the remaining passenger, in the seat directly opposite the cameraman, Andy felt almost numbed by the predictability. The passenger was, inevitably, a slim young blond in a ripped t-shirt and jeans who, equally inevitably, would prove to have no ticket and no money. Then Andy suddenly sat up and looked more attentively. The blond was Kieran Radford.

He smiled up at the ticket-collector, who was side-on to the camera, in a pleading puppyish way, but it was clear that the black guy meant to have his clothes in part-payment a least. Kieran stripped off and then with a deft move - it must have been years of practice with fare-dodgers - the ticket-collector pushed Kieran onto his knees

147

with one hand and unzipped his trousers with the other. Kieran set about his task as if he were embarking on a well-buttered corn-on-the-cob, and soon the two me from the other end of the compartment crowded in. Thereafter, it all became a shade confused, and it ended with unseemly haste. Perhaps they were approaching a station. It did, after all, seem to be an entirely real train.

'He'll do anything to be photographed,' Philpotts had said when Andy showed him his snaps. Now Andy saw what he meant.

✷ ✷ ✷

Kieran had slept the long, deep and unexpectedly dream-less sleep of the exhausted and the wounded. Waking towards noon, he was puzzled and almost dismayed to find himself slightly bruised but otherwise physically uninjured apart from a strange bitter taste, like a residue of all his suppressed fear, in the mouth. There was little food in the place - Kieran believed in eating real meals wherever possible in restaurants or other people's flats, even when he cooked them himself - but he managed to find bread, cheese and a blotchy tomato. Then he went out into the world. The South London sky had a veiled, creamily unhealthy look about it: the state of the summer, the state of the city, was terminal. He walked purposefully to the nearest MegaGlobe travel agent who managed without difficulty to book him onto a flight for Copenhagen the following morning and who accepted without curiosity his debit card payment. After that, he went in search of a phone, miraculously finding one in Stockwell Road which was both operative and unoccupied.

'Philpotts!' The voice, thought Kieran, sounded uncharacteristically weary.

'Hello dear, it's Kieran. Listen, I'm in a call-box, so I'll have to be quick. They've cut off the phone at home.'

'Kieran, how marvellous to hear you. You're in a call-boy, you say? Anyway, are you all right?'

'Yes, of course, I'm indestructible, remember? But listen,

148

I've decided to put your kindness to good use and go away for a little while. There seems to be some trouble brewing, and it might make sense to be somewhere where it isn't.'

'Quite, quite.' Philpotts seemed unsurprised. As if to explain his muted reaction he added: 'And remember I told you *that*, last week. Where are you going?'

'Copenhagen. I've got some friends there I can stay with, and I've managed to get a seat on a flight tomorrow. I'll send you a postcard from the Tivoli Gardens. Or the Pan Club.'

'I'll look forward to that.'

'Good, but anyway, how are you? You sound a bit subdued.'

'Oh, a little down, you know. Nothing that won't pass. You're sure you're all right?'

'Yes, dear, I'm *all right*.' His pennies were ticking away. 'Must go now. Take care, dear, and thanks for everything.'

He put the phone down and thought about ringing Clive. He knew he didn't actually want to see Clive. He also knew that he didn't want to see him because he loved him, and that Clive wouldn't find - wouldn't want to find - this easy to understand. Clive, given half a chance, would start to ache with affection in his neurotic, protective way, and Kieran couldn't take that: he needed simply to disappear for a bit, a need that even Clive, at phone's length, might just possibly understand. He dialled the number.

'The number you are calling has been changed....,' began a disembodied voice.

'No it fucking hasn't,' said Kieran to the phone, before slamming it down and dialling again.

'Hello, Greenslade Graphics,' Clive answered. He was in the studio, then. In the domestic part of the flat he answered as Clive Greenslade; at his desk, depending on whether he was closer to typewriter or Letraset, he became in business hours, self-mockingly, 'Greenslade Literary Services' or 'Greenslade Graphics'.

'Hello Greenslade Graphics, it's Radford Rent-a-Boy,' said Kieran with a juantiness that didn't fool either of them.

'Kieran.' He heard the momentary speechlessness. 'I've been trying to phone you. Where are you? Are you okay? Your phone....'

'Yes dear, I'm fine. The phone's cut off because the world's a pig, and I'm in a callbox somewhere in SW9.'

'Well I'm glad you're somewhere anyway. Look, we must have a talk. Can we meet? I know I'll see you at the Poetry Society tomorrow evening but this is a bit urgent.'

'I hope it's not about close encounters with pretty policemen.'

'Why?'

'Because you know that leather boy from Saturday aternoon?'

'Yes, he was in the Clarendon the other night.'

'What? Did he do anything to you?'

'No, just a friendly warning from his mates.'

'Thank god for that. He picked me up. In The Pit. I've got the scars to prove it.'

'Kieran, not seriously?'

'Not the scars, don't worry. I'm not hurt. But I do think things are about to turn a bit nasty, and I'm going to disappear for a few days.'

'Where?'

'Copenhagen. It's okay, Philpotts, bless him, has given me the cash. I'm off tomorrow, so I shan't make it to the Poetry Society, I'm afraid.'

'Can we meet sometime today then?'

'Probably better not, dear. You know how it is. Such sweet sorrow, and all that. I shan't be gone long, in any case. And I'll send you a postcard from the Tivoli Gardens. Or the Cosy Bar.'

'Well, take care. I think I'll get out of London for a few days myself. I promised Jeremy I'd try to get to Suffolk this weekend, and I may as well go tomorrow now.'

'Good, then you can send me a postcard too. Listen, my money's running out. I'll see you soon. Promise.'

As he was speaking, a red car screeched to a standstill at the kerb. A rough-looking spiky-haired boy leapt from the

150

passenger seat, ran round to the back of the car, opened the boot, and took from an overnight bag a small tasselled leather-covered cosh which he shoved up his sleeve before jumping back into his seat and slamming the door. The car sped away again, its occupants laughing and shouting. For a terrified instant Kieran had thought it might be the guys from RAID again. He supposed he'd been lucky: he had, after all, heard the stories - truncheons, whips, electric shocks, it couldn't possibly be true. The red car had vanished; all the same, it was an odd incident, unsettling and purposelessly nasty. What was going on?

Kieran walked aimlessly along the tired streets: it was as if someone had turned the contrast down, this milky-skied light. He felt unfitted, out of place. There were days when a sideways look from a scrappy old London pigeon could be disquieting, and this was one of them. Even the rubbish on the pavement couldn't summon the energy to blow about in its usual ankle-slapping way: instead it gently levitated and fell back, sighing, on itself. Crazily anachronistic, an elderly man in a bowler hat was hailing a bus as if he imagined it to be a taxi, as if he imagined himself to be in the city of fifty years ago.

After a while Kieran found himself approaching Kennington Park. The northern end, where the march had finished on Saturday, was now occupied by a silent funfair: it seemed to offer a quirky sort of sanctuary, so Kieran crossed the road and began to wander among the stalls. There were a few unconcened people putting finishing touches to things - the fair was evidently due to open later that afternoon - but no-one took any notice of him. A huge old man who looked like a geological outcrop was optimistically opening up his sweet stall: 'FRANK ROBSON THE ROCK KING,' it said, 'FOR TRADITIONAL BOILINGS.' It sounded like an image from the underworld - you were never, it seemed, far from that in London these days. An entirely shuttered stall exhorted the public in bright infantile colours, to 'WIN A SAFARI BEAR.' 'Safari chicken,' thought Kieran. 'Bear coop. Polar chicken. Tandori bear.' A little further on, another stall

151

invited him to 'WIN A CAVEMAN.' That seemed more like it, but on closer inspection the cavemen in question proved to be gormless little gonks. A couple of doubtful men were wandering round a Noah's Ark roundabout, apparently making sure that the animals were firmly screwed down. Above each exit there was a painted sentence in which random capitalised words seemed to turn practical instructions into opaque moral dicta. 'It's SAFE as long as you're SEATED' was, out of context, simply misleading, but 'Wait until ride STOPS before GETTING OFF' had a more universal application. A lanky long-haired youth was setting up a labyrinth of fruit machines, some of which were standing around at odd angles, winking and flashing deliriously. Kieran stood watching the complex yet entirely mindless progress of the coloured lights, blurring in and out of focus. He felt dizzy, vaguely disembodied though quite relaxed.

'Bright lights always cheat you in the end,' he said. He didn't know why: after all, he liked bright lights.

'Sorry?' said the lanky youth, indifferently: he held a fistful of cables in one hand and an electrical screwdriver in the other, and he glanced from one to the other as if between them they might provide the answer to some momentous problem. Then he looked more sharply at Kieran. 'You all right?'

'Yes, fine,' said Kieran, swaying slightly.

'You don't look all right. Would you like a drink? Coffee?'

'Yes, coffee would be fine.'

'Come on, I'm due for a break. I'll finish this lot in a bit.' He led the way beyond the stalls to a caravan. It was full of cheap nomadic furniture and philosophy books.

'Dylan!' said Kieran.

'Sorry?'

'Just a coincidence - another philosopher who's a bit like you. You're a philosophy student?'

'Almost. I've been doing this sort of thing for a year, but I'm starting a degree in October.' He switched on a filter machine. 'Can't stand fairground coffee, though. I guess

152

that's what's really driving me to university.'

'It'll be quite a change. Or maybe not. I mean, a travelling fair must throw up all kinds of images and ideas which you can use.'

The philosopher laughed appreciatively. 'You're absolutely right. It's a totally artificial environment which in one way makes no pretence to reality, and yet at the same time the fairground is like a parody of the city, this caravan's a parody of home, and the whole thing's constantly trundling off to new places so that every fourth or fifth day the reality outside the fair alters completely while the illusion retains its crazy consistency. At least it does if I can get those bloody machines to work.'

'And if all that stuff outside *is* reality. If this world remains constant and predictable whereas everything else keeps changing, there must be a strong philosophical case for arguing that this is what's real and the other's some kind of mirage.'

'A case, but not a strong one. It all depends on where you're standing at the time. Anyway, don't forget that philosophy is a species of self-induced madness, as some unusually self-aware though probably loony professor pointed out.'

'And that saying what you mean isn't always, or often, they same as meaning what you say.'

'Exactly. You're not a philosophy student yourself?'

'No, a penniless poet, a character in search of an author or an author in search of a character, a creative layabout.'

'*Deraciné.*'

'Unrooted, uprooted.'

'Either.'

'Yes, it's strange. Among people I know I'd say I was unrooted, a free agent. But it isn't altogether true. I want to shape the world even as I'm cutting myself off from it.'

'A classic twentieth century dilemma. You should try working in a fair. And read Camus.'

'God,' said Kieran, 'I should read so much. I've been trying to get through some nineteenth century French fiction - Balzac, Flaubert - but I never seem to find the

153

time. Or at least, not the right kind of time and space. And it's an odd consequence of being, I don't know, passably articulate that other people constantly assume you're well-informed, well-read. You pick up all kinds of smatterings of learning second-hand, when really you hardly know who you are yourself. I don't know why I'm telling you all this.'

'Probably because you don't know who I am either. How do you like your coffee?'

'As it comes, black, sugarless.'

'Just as well. I haven't got any proper milk.'

There was a sudden hammering on the door of the caravan, which then burst open to reveal a man apparently hewn from the same lump of stone as Frank Robson The Rock King. 'What the fuck do you think you're doing?' he said, ignoring Kieran, who felt gratefully invisible. 'You're s'posed to be setting up the fruiters. Y'know, the orchard on wheels?'

'Okay, I'm coming.' The philosopher added patiently, as if to an elderly relative which perhaps, amazingly, he was, 'I'll bring my coffee with me.' He grinned at Kieran, pouring coffee into two mugs. 'Here's yours. And here's Camus: have a look at it.' He chucked a paperback copy of *The Outsider*. 'If you leave before I get back, make sure the door locks behind you.'

'Thanks,' said Kieran. 'That's really kind.'

Kieran propped himself up on the bunk and started to read: he'd try at least to get far enough to outlast the coffee and to offer some suitably informed comment to the philosopher with the fruit machines when he left. But he was soon dozing, and he heard without surprise or concern the familiar sound of a book falling from his hands.

He dreamed, as he did recurrently, that he was being pursued down a long flight of stairs. Above him was a curved segmented ceiling which he soon recognised with slight relief as that of a Piccadilly Line escalator; but there was no-one, apart from himself and the pursuer towards whom he dared not turn, on the unmoving staircase. Suddenly he became aware of a busker at the foot of the

154

stairs. He was playing 'Summertime' on a flute, except that the flute had somehow acquired the shape of a vast monstrous tuba, the bell of which was entirely blocking Kieran's path: if he kept on running he must actually jump into the instrument. He steeled himself to do so and, as often happens in dreams, the obstacle melted beneath the force of his will-power. He found himself on an empty and darkened station platform, still with the sense of a pursuer behind him. A train approached, slowing but failing to stop until it had vanished once more into the tunnel; then, however, it reversed so that the last door of the last carriage opened onto the platform. Kieran dashed gratefully in and so, as the doors slid together, did whoever was chasing him. Dreams have their own logic, their crystalline congruence, and he would have been unnerved by a sense of dream-logic betrayed if the person who now sat down opposite him had been other than Andy Symes. Andy smiled encouragingly and produced a pair of handcuffs from his leather jacket. 'Shall we go?' he said. 'But where?' asked Kieran; they were, after all, on a moving train between stations. 'I know a place,' said Andy. Kieran held his hands out willingly, submissively, but Andy snapped one handcuff onto Kieran's right wrist and the other onto his own left wrist. The doors slid open onto a long-deserted platform. 'I know where this is,' Kieran thought, in a self slightly outside the dream, 'it's one of those lost tube stations, like the one that's supposed to be under that masonic place in Great Queen Street.' 'It's Gloucester Road while it was closed,' suggested another voice. 'Hi,' said Andy to someone in the shadows, 'glad you could make it.' Julian's friend Kevin stepped forward and handcuffed Kieran's other wrist to his own. They walked forward, Kieran between them. 'I feel like Alice between the two queens,' he said, but neither of them seemed to notice. In front of them in the darkness there were coloured lights, and the sounds of a crowd began to seep through the air of a warm summer night. It was - of course - the Tivoli Gardens in Copenhagen, and here was Clive walking towards them. They kissed, but could hardly embrace. 'My dear,' said Kieran, 'I'm a bit tied up at present. As you see.' He felt detached and elated, carried along by the boys and the noise, the crowds and the coloured lights. Then he slowly opened his eyes to see through the windows of the caravan the lights of a South London fairground. He sighed, and turned the sigh into a shrug. He found an old cash machine advice slip and scribbled 'Thanks again' on it before tucking it inside the paperback Camus and closing the door carefully behind him as he left.

SEVEN

He was driving as hard as he could, in the fast lane of the M3, waiting for the moment when Capital would stammer into range on the car radio. It was Andy's own car, his old hammered XR3, and these days it seemed the nearest thing to home he possessed. Even its familiar rattles and the immodest roar of its derelict silencer were reassuring, and this morning he needed reassurance. The evening and night hadn't been a great success. Straight away he'd seen that Debbie was at her most distant and serious: his clumsy instinct had been to take her to the most expensive restaurant he could afford, hoping for some transformation while beginning to experience that familiar, ominous knotting-up inside which soon had him longing for a pint of lager in a cheap crowded pub. Somewhere near the beginning of the main course he'd nagged her into telling him, as if he wasn't already wildly guessing, what was wrong. She was pregnant, she said, so softly that everyone in the room knew that something momentous had been uttered: it would have been more tactful to shout it. Andy thought, uselessly, of calculated risks which in retrospect had been simply risks. He thought of what his parents and his father's parishoners would say, and him the vicar's son. He couldn't bring himself to think of Debbie, or the putative child, at all. They had gone home to her dreadful digs, tiptoed up the stairs and gone to bed with all the nervous circumspection of fugitive schoolchildren. In the morning, when he had left her half-asleep, they both wondered whether he was leaving her for good.

He stopped for breakfast at a motorway service area and scanned the headlines on other people's papers. Adjacent readers seemed to inhabit almost literally different worlds: 'STERLING CRISIS TRIGGERS NEW INTEREST RATE FEAR' was the most significant matter in one man's universe this morning, 'ALIENS RAPED MY GOLDFISH' dominated another's world-picture. He drove on, hard in the fast lane, breezily ignoring the 50 mph speed limit around some insignificant roadworks until, a mile or so later, the blue lights and siren overtook him and signalled him onto the hard shoulder. There they were, the two of them, smug chummy little traffic cops, older than Andy but with no ambition to become Metropolitan Police Commissioner or even to break an IRA man. He flashed his ID card at them, but they didn't seem especially impressed. One of them did a slow critical circuit of the car before returning to the driver's window.

'This your own car, sir?'

'Yes.'

'Rear offside tyre's a bit dodgy, I'd say. I should get that seen to if I were you.'

'Thanks for the advice. Anything else?'

'Yes,' said the other one. 'If you want to drive like a complete prat in future, do it on your own patch will you? Saves phone calls and paperwork.'

Andy hadn't properly recovered from this when he arrived at the office an hour later. He went straight to the top floor, brushing aside both the ghosts of nineteenth century grocers and the more solid forms of twentieth century policemen, and crashed into Angela's office. She looked up at him with an ironic, unsurprised smile.

'You're bright and early.'

'Early. Anything for me?'

'Yes, three things. Inspector Clarke's at a meeting but he left you this warrant and said when you've done that would you have a look at this file.'

'What is it?'

'IRA. A new North London lead he wants you to investigate. Looks like it could be the big one for you.'

'Great. Initiative rewarded - makes a change. What was the third thing?'

'Oh,' Angela grinned, 'a complaint from Hampshire Constabulary about your driving.'

'Pigs.'

'Yes. Aren't they?'

'I suppose they've just got their first fax machine and want to show off. Can I have a car and a driver to do this warrant?'

'That's a bit grand, isn't it?'

'Not really. It could be a political, questions in the House one, so we'd better do it in style. Besides, I'd like someone else there to see that I observe the proper formalities. I'm getting worried about my reputation.'

'Why, what have you been up to?'

It was Andy's turn to grin. 'Driving too fast.'

'Well.' Angela consulted a screen and a desk diary, and tried to make it look like a momentous concession. 'I can spare you Trevor if you're quick. The boss is going to need him at 10.30.'

'Fine, can you fix it? I'll meet him downstairs in five minutes.'

He hurtled out of the office and slammed his fist on the hot drink machine in the corridor. He was sure he'd hit the coffee-with-everything button, but a plastic cup containing half an inch of cold chicken soup fell out. He hadn't time to waste with the lift, so he raced down the stairs and flung the IRA file on his desk. There were some odds and ends, routine confetti, in his in-tray, but they could wait. Some miserable sod had been in and pinched the tv and video, but who cared now? At last they were letting him loose on terrorists: it must have been that brilliant stroke of luck with Philpotts which had swung things with Clarke. In a few short months he'd graduated from standard Old Bill stuff with crooks in Cortinas through the pinko-political underworld to the real action. He felt good, and if he'd had those Hampshire coppers in front of him now he'd have told them what to do with their truncheons, or done it for them. He strode into the underground car-park to meet dour, ageless Trevor, useful ballast in a scrum but the face of unpromotable reliability.

'Hi, Trev,' he said, getting into the red Astra. '24 Swinburne Gardens, SW 10. Take it away, Starsky.'

But as the streets of West London flashed by in the drab

159

sunless light, his temporary exhilaration left him. Debbie and the baby. Marriage. It was something he'd never seriously begun to consider, but he knew she'd want to have the child, and if she still wanted him too she'd want marriage. So would his father. So probably would Inspector Clarke and the faceless hierarchy: after all, if your professional life was as dubious as Andy's, your private life had to be impeccable. That was one of the rules, in fact it was almost the only rule: you spent your life at RAID wading into muck, but there mustn't be the slightest speck to throw at you personally, ever. The press and the public, the great authoritarian silent majority, would turn on you at once at destroy you completely. It was the only sense in which Andy felt that his job closely resembled his father's.

They were heading off Brompton Road towards Swinburne Gardens. He needed to steady himself.

'Got a joke for you, Trev,' he said. 'I used to be a paedophile, but the cunt split on me.' The twitch on Trevor's face couldn't really be called a smile. 'Oh all right, please yourself. Hey, wait a bit, what's going on here? Let me out and get back to me when you've found somewhere to park this thing. I don't believe this. More bloody bluebottles.'

There was a patrol car artlessly parked outside 24 Swinburne Gardens, and the door of the house was wide open. Andy could hardly bear the thought: some uniformed fool from the local nick had got in first and done Philpotts for some trivial offence without any suspicion of the great web Andy had been spinning. It couldn't be. It had to be one of the other flats - the Fairhavens or the mysterious Rick.

He strode up the steps. There was no-one in the huge featureless hall, but Philpotts' own door was ajar. Andy walked in, slowed now by the silence which was broken only by irregular half-stifled gasps, like the tail-end of sobbing. In the kitchen at the end of the passage he could glimpse the little Italian woman, Francesca, sitting pallid and hunched. In the doorway of the living-room, alerted

160

by Andy's approaching footsteps, stood Greg Thornton.

'What the fuck,' Andy hissed, 'are you doing here? And where's Philpotts?'

Greg beckoned him deeper into the room, and closed the door behind them. 'Philpotts is in the bedroom,' he said. 'He's dead. His housekeeper found him and phoned the ambulance and the police. That's why I'm here.'

'Then where's the bloody ambulance?'

'Hasn't arrived yet.'

'You must have got here bloody fast. What were you doing? Waiting on the doorstep for a chance to screw up one of my cases?'

'I was a couple of streets away - some bloke chained and beaten up by a bit of rough, by the look of it. And a very expensive camera smashed all over him. It's a strange morning.'

'Okay, okay. You're sure he's dead? Why, how?'

'Two bottles of Margaux, one bottle of pills. It's a smart way to O/D.'

'Fuck, and fuck again. Is there a note?'

'There's more than a note.' At this moment a WPC put her head round the door. 'In the kitchen,' Greg said. 'Thanks.'

'More?' Without knowing precisely why, Andy suddenly felt very worried indeed - not least by Greg's manner, which was beginning to seem far less deferential and far more knowing than it had any right to be. Power was ebbing away from Andy, and relics of the earlier relationship between them were resurfacing. 'What sort of more?'

'I think you should have a look at his desk. You were obviously meant to.'

'*Meant* to?' Aware that he was sounding like an idiotic echo, Andy crossed to the desk. It was neatly arranged: it was, indeed, meant to be seen. On the right hand side were two sealed envelopes of good quality laid paper. One was stamped and addressed to Kieran Radford. The other, unstamped, simply bore the words 'Sgt Andrew Symes'. The careful scholarly hand was all too familiar to him. On the left hand side of the desk was the carbon copy of a typed letter, plainly one of several such letters stacked beneath it and surmounted altogether too perkily by the bronze paperweight. The letter, addressed to the editor of *The Guardian*, was a vividly eloquent protest about the persecution which he, an elderly and distinguished homosexual, was being subjected to by a shadowy new branch of the police force. The date was underlined in red felt-tip pen. Andy stared at that, mildly puzzled for a moment.

'He wants you to note the date,' Greg explained, 'so that you'll know he posted them yesterday. They could be in tomorrow's papers.'

'Shit. He's planned it like the end of some bloody tragedy.'

'I'd say a scene featuring a corpse and an upstaged copper had more in common with farce. You don't know Joe Orton?'

'Another poofter.'

'But essential reading for policemen.'

'Reading isn't an occupation we encourage among police officers. We try to keep the paper work down to a minimum.'

'Bloody hell. So you do know Orton?'

'Only that quote.'

'Better than nothing. Anyway, what are you going to do with your letter?'

'Read it. Some time.'

'And the other one? You're obviously meant to react to that too, otherwise he'd have posted it along with the ones to the press.'

Andy had, in fact, been about to open it. 'I'm going to post it. It can't do me any more harm. Anyway, he's out of the country.'

'Who is?'

'Kieran Radford.'

'Whoever he may be. When did he go?'

'Today. Sometime today.'

'That must be the other reason why he left the letter unposted, then. He didn't want this Radford to get it before leaving.'

'Okay. And I suppose my own letter will tell me that.'

'There's only one way to find out. You'll look much more suspicious if you refuse to open a letter addressed to yourself than if you do open it.'

Andy carefully opened the envelope. The letter was quite short.

'Dear Sergeant Symes,' it said. 'I hope you will forgive me for inconveniencing you, though it will be rather obvious that you have seriously inconvenienced me. I have made my views on your activities plain in letters to the editors of a number of newspapers today, but these are general rather than personal observations. You are, however, personally responsible for some things: Kieran Radford's temporary exile, for one. I do not wish him to receive his letter (next to this one on my desk) before he leaves: it contains, as they say, information which may prove to his advantage - financially, that is - and receiving it might delay his departure. I intend it to be good news on his return, and you would do me a kindness (which I am afraid you certainly owe me) by posting it. Please, however, do not feel that you are personally responsible for my decision to shuffle off, etc.; you are not (yet) as important or as powerful as that. I had considered the matter for months, years. It was simply a matter of timing. It always is. Yours sincerely, R. Bertram Philpotts.'

'Damn him,' said Andy.

'Everything explained?'

'Enough. Looks like I've screwed it all up.'

Greg glanced round the placid bookish room and then looked steadily at Andy. 'I don't think so,' he said. 'Speaking simply as a friend, I don't think you were ever quite important enough to screw it *all* up.'

'That's what Philpotts said.'

'Well, I wouldn't know about him. I've only met him as a corpse, but I suppose I can judge him a bit by his artefacts. And by his style. He looks to me to have been a tough-minded intelligent old buffer who knew exactly what he was up to and was just looking for the right catalyst. He must have regarded you rather as Cleopatra regarded the asp.'

'What?'

'Means to an end. No, you couldn't have screwed it up, though I'd guess he may have made life difficult for you.'

'You're not kidding.'

'I'm not, and neither was he.'

There was a mild commotion in the hall, which Andy at first took to be simply the WPC directing the ambulance crew to Philpotts' bedroom, but which turned out to include a breathless Trevor as epilogue. He stumbled unceremoniously into the room.

'Inspector Clarke wants you back at base,' he said. 'Sounds urgent. He's had the press on the phone about something. Whatever it is, he's not pleased.'

'You go on back,' said Andy. 'This guy'll give me a lift. I'll be there as soon as I've finished here.'

Trevor looked horrified. 'Are you sure? I mean....' Andy knew exactly what he meant.

'Yes, I'm sure. Now fuck off back to the grocery.'

Trevor fled wordlessly from the room.

'That wasn't...,' Greg began, then corrected himself. 'I was going to say, "That wasn't like you" - but of course it was. Exactly like you, for a change.'

'Well, if I'm going to be sacked in half an hour, I'm damned if I'm going to spend the time getting there with a donkey like that. I need someone with a few brain cells to help me prepare the speech for the defence. Though I'm not sure now that the whole business is even worth defending. Can you manage a detour to Hammersmith?'

'Yes, of course. There's hardly anything left to do. I've got the notes I need for my report, and I'll just go and have a quick word with WPC Fuller to make sure the house-keeper's all right. Do you want to have a look round?'

'It's your case,' said Andy, struggling to produce an uneasy smile.

'You forget that I don't really know what *your* case was going to be about. And I don't expect you to tell me. I'll be back in a moment.'

164

Andy looked out of the window, across Swinburne Gardens and down the turning opposite. There was row upon row of these solid stuccoed houses, each one sliced horizontally into flats, each flat containing separate secret lives which would translate, with scarcely a moment's warning, into separate secret deaths. The sheer particularity of it was terrifying. And as for the incidental details.... He looked down at the window-box, packed lavishly with geraniums and petunias. Who would water them now? Who would care whether they were watered or not?

He turned back towards the room, his mind spinning but luminous, as if at the unstoppable optimum moment of drunkenness in which everything makes sense before all becomes nonsense. There was something here he needed to understand. He gazed at the books, thousands of them, on Philpotts' shelves, and felt sadly that understanding might take time and patience he didn't possess. One book - a Shakespeare play by the look of it - lay propped open at its final pages where someone, presumably Philpotts, had underlined a few sentences in pencil: 'A goodly medicine for my aching bones! O world, world, world! Thus is the poor agent despised.'

'I've found the note,' said Andy, when Greg returned.

'I thought we'd got that already.'

'No, this is the real one. Look.'

'He *was* a mischievous old bugger, wasn't he?' Greg said admiringly, when he'd glanced at the book. 'He'd just been to see a production of *Troilus and Cressida* - there's a theatre programme on his bedside table - but I'd hardly have thought of him as Pandarus. Still, he obviously wasn't one to resist a literary joke. I wonder what'll happen to his books.'

'I think I can guess.'

'The mysterious Kieran Radford? Does he deserve them?'

'How the fuck do I know?' Andy flung himself furiously onto the sofa. 'I may not have been important enough to screw it all up, but I've got it all wrong.'

'Go on.'

'Oh well, it's all too absurdly obvious now. I just couldn't see what's important. All the porn and stuff I was messing about with - it's not what these serious people take seriously, even when they're tangled up in it. It's not what matters. For people like Philpotts, or even Radford, what I've been looking at is all on the surface, it's part of them but it's only a kind of veneer: their real selves are somewhere I wasn't getting to. Everything I've been chasing is just unreal.'

'So you'd better not forget to post Radford's letter. It sounds as if he does deserve to get the books.'

'Probably. When I first asked Philpotts about him, he said that he was a highly intelligent and promising writer - something like that, anyway. And he meant it, I think. I mean, that was the important thing about him. If for Philpotts the important thing about Radford had been "He's a sexy little bastard who models for porn magazines and videos", he'd have said so. But it wasn't, and he didn't. Do you see what I'm getting at?'

'Yes, I think so.'

'I wasn't just playing the wrong game, I was playing the wrong sort of game. I wasn't seeing that the big moral issues are in the end tied up with real detail. After all, we all have weird sex lives and weirder fantasies, so it's crazy to get excited about that. What's more important is who's going to water those fucking geraniums now?'

'Or whatever.'

'Yes, Greg, or whatever. By the way, Debbie's pregnant.'

'Ah, I see. That sort of whatever. What will you do?'

'At this moment, I'd like to move to Scotland and have a croft.'

'Like Paul McCartney.'

'No, like me.'

'It'll be a change from Hammersmith. Shall we go?'

'Can't we go for a drink first?'

'Hardly, I'm on duty.'

'You know what?'

'What?'

'You sound just like a fucking policeman.'

*　*　*

Packing, Kieran found, was paradoxically easier when you didn't know how long you were likely to be away. Fixed periods could cause minute, complex calculations about shirts and socks and underwear - especially, in the more hectic phases of his life, the latter - to say nothing of toothpaste and razorblades, pills and Prioderm, just in case. This was different, it was indeed more like a proper holiday. All he could do was to assemble as much as was clean and wearable and stuffable into a bag and go. Before that, though, there were a few other things to be done.

For a start, he must leave a note for his landlord. Kieran was in fact supposed to be looking after the house for its owner, an itinerant musician presently occupied at some obscure but doubtless sunny European festival, as well as feeding the cat, Minim. The fact that Minim, who despite his kittenish name had grown into a large tabby of uncertain temperament, seldom came home these days, having found more socially reliable providers than Kieran, was largely beside the point. This morning, as if acting on secret information, Minim had lollopped nonchalantly through the flap in the back door and he now sat pretending to lick his left front paw but really eyeing Kieran across the kitchen table. 'Dear Richard,' Kieran wrote, on a postcard of Caravaggio's *Boy Bitten by a Lizard*, 'I've got to go away for a few days but I'll probably be back before you read this (in which case you won't read this). The gas and electricity are OFF but the water is ON - it's not going to freeze, is it? If by any chance I'm delayed I'll send you a (i.e. another) postcard. Don't worry about Minim - he's alive and disgustingly well, and Mrs R at No 47 is feeding him. Hope you've had a good time, and anyway where's *your* postcard? Love, Kieran.' At this Minim sneezed, twice.

Then there was Bertram Philpotts to consider. There had been two items in the post for Kieran this morning: a rejection-slip from a poetry magazine in Huddersfield and a jiffy-bag from Philpotts. The latter contained two books - *Poems, 1938* and *The Golden Key* - by William Brannigan, in copies affectionately inscribed to Bertram Philpotts, together with a note and another loose sheet of paper. 'Kieran - You might like to have these, to keep of course, as I don't suppose I'll have any further use for them. Clearing out some papers I also came across a poem Brannigan sent me much later, in his lighthouse-keeper phase I should imagine. It really isn't any *good* at all - he must have wanted it to look like unrhymed syllabics, which I never cared for, but he couldn't be bothered to count properly. However, it's an oddity, and presumably unique. Why do so many poets feel compelled to write these melancholic aubades? I'm buggered if I know. Take care - RBP.'

The poem was typed on creamish quarto paper, using an old manual machine on which the letter 'e' was coming seriously adrift. It was certainly, Kieran agreed, a curiosity.

Aubade

Images of the landscape that we remember best
    confound our tomorrows. The North Sea was violent
that winter; sleet shattered on the window-sill and fell,
    melting, to the running earth. There were no gulls.
The sun awoke early in the water each morning,
    and by noon the sky was black, the horizon
too dangerously clear. On most days Zeus, after
    a sleepless night, found his egg was hard, and sent
thunder: but I do not ask you to remember that,
    it is all too near and too distant. The best
we can ever do is to say, 'That tree reminds me...'
    and leave the phrase unfinished (details never
matter for long in any case). You will never know
    why these things remain, nor I expect you to.
All I ask is that on the journey we are taking
    I should be the guide, and that you will pretend
not to notice the wrong turnings. The road is narrow
    here, as narrow as the seaside village streets,

> smelling of fish and yesterday's women, where the
>   dawn
>   comes suddenly across the waking water,

He wondered about that careless comma, unable to decide whether it signalled a Gravesian joke or mere incompleteness: probably the latter, he thought. After reading the poem through a couple of times, he decided to phone Philpotts: the books, at any rate, were an extraordinarily generous gift. The phone in the house seemed this morning to have been reconnected: perhaps the boys from RAID thought he'd already left or else, knowing that he was on his way, no longer cared abut him. Bertram's number rang and rang. It wasn't like him to be out so early, but he'd been behaving a bit oddly in the last few days. Kieran decided to try again from Heathrow if he had time.

There remained the routine chores which must precede his departure: rubbish-bins and wastepaper-baskets to be emptied, stains to be removed, cutlery and utensils on the draining-board to be put away. He knew that Richard on his return would obsessively pick up stray details: a scribbled note on the pad by the phone, a cigarette-end of the wrong brand, an unfamiliar till receipt - anything like that could start him off on some wild speculation. So Kieran went over the house, cleaning, emptying, double-checking, while Minim danced uncharacteristically skittish attentions around him.

Since Tuesday night, Kieran had wandered around South London in a kind of disoriented daze: the fairground was the furthest he'd strayed from home. Now, too late, he began to discover things he might usefully have done in that slab of wasted time. He could, for instance, have spent a reassuring few hours taping music for his journey from Richard's record collection. Though given to uncharacteristic sternness in his public views on music, Kieran was as ever happy to bend or break the rules for his private pleasures: once he had assembled - and long since erased, in case someone stumbled upon it - a tape of his favourite slow movements from Mahler, ending of course with the final movement of the ninth, by which point Kieran would be drenched with emotion. Today he had to settle for what was readily at hand: some favourite symphonies, bumptious bits and all, and Jessye Norman's recording of the *Four Last Songs*.

Sooner than he'd thought, it was time to leave: Minim, sensing desertion in the air, had already disappeared through the cat-flap and doubtless made his way back to Mrs R's elderly hospitality. Kieran slung out a full dustbin bag without much confidence that it would ever actually get collected - you simply never knew these days - then went indoors for the last time to collect his luggage. He supposed he'd be back, sooner or later.

Although it was only mid-morning, the day seemed overtired. The streets were muffled and stunned, the Northern Line populated only by people who'd forgotten where they were going or why. When he changed to the Piccadilly, the old buzz, muted but inevitable as instinct, distantly filtered through: could there ever have been a boy from the North who hadn't dreamed of Leicester Square and Piccadilly Circus as the star turns in a great network of urban pleasures? And, Kieran wondered, could there ever have been a boy who, having discovered London, hadn't longed to trade it for the more honest raunchiness of Amsterdam or Copenhagen? Unashamedly as ever, he studied the boys on the tube, the boots, the scuffed trainers, the ripped and faded jeans, the vests and t-shirts, all the symbols of good, messy metropolitan sexiness; and then the drawn, pallid faces, the bagged eyes, the suppressed sadness that seemed to speak of a city which was really no fun anymore. A detached line drifted into his mind: 'I had not thought death had undone so many.' Strange how you could always tell a tourist from say Holland or Denmark by the liveliness of the eyes, just as you could so often, conversely, identify the Englishman abroad.

At Earl's Court he almost, intuitively, made for the door, suddenly realising that he should have left an hour earlier and called on Bertram personally to thank him for his gift. Now, there simply wasn't time, and soon the train was blundering through the anonymities of West London: when, towards Hammersmith, it began to poke its nose tentatively above ground, it seemed to Kieran an impertinence, almost an affront - the Piccadilly Line was a creature of darkness which ought to shun daylight. Somewhere near here, Andy Symes was busy in his basement concocting the tabloid headline-making story which, by stupidly smearing Martin Baxter, would nevertheless keep the government ahead in the ratings for a while yet. Kieran didn't give a toss about Martin, who was after all a politician and deserved everything he got, and he in fact secretly regretted that he wouldn't be around to relish his own infamous part in the supposed scandal, but he was extremely sorry that he had been unwittingly turned into a prop for any sort of government - least of all this one. Thinking this, he delivered himself of a little pouting sigh. That was all it was worth.

He found himself reflecting on the featureless suburbia of West London. For a while he'd known someone who'd lived in one of those unspeakable places, Rayner's Lane it had been, and who had found it impossible, after weeks if not months, to set off for home with the confidence of reaching it. It wasn't just the uniformity of a sprawling estate - you could come across that anywhere - it was the way in which all human ambience seemed to have been syphoned out of the place, so that there was no *point* in remembering which road was which. For Kieran, that was far closer to an image of hell than anything he'd had to suffer his week. He looked at his watch. They were at Hounslow Central, and time was getting tight. There wouldn't after all be a chance to phone Bertram.

Eventually they slid into Heathrow and for the last time Kieran left the familiar, comforting world of the Piccadilly Line behind him. The airport terminal crowd was less reassuring, laden either with businesslike composure or touristy panic. Kieran grinned sourly to himself: even in this international gateway, grime and graffiti were taking over like a peculiarly English fungus. Once there'd been those chirpy signs which read 'Say Hello to the Good Buys at Heathrow'; now some joker had inscribed on a wall, indelibly it seemed, 'Say Good Bye to the Hell at Heathrow'. That was about right. As he jostled his way among the other passengers in search of information, a disembodied resonant crone was starting to announce his flight: 'Passengers for flight SK 581 to Copenhagen....' Kieran moved on eagerly; Bertram, bless his soul, would be proud of him.

And England? England could fuck itself.

* * *

Every time Clive drove into East Anglia, they seemed to have moved Ipswich. Once, Ipswich had been just a dumb obstacle to be negotiated, easily if slowly: a predictable sequence of roundabouts and traffic-lights through the unmistakably dull outskirts of a large town. Now, a new road swept you east of the place and over the Orwell Bridge, and if you were unwary halfway to Felixstowe before you realised what was wrong. Today at least he got that right, noting with cautious optimism that there were a few hints of brightness at last in the sallow sky over towards the coast. His cheerfulness didn't last long. Before he could rejoin the road he actually remembered north of Ipswich, he was flagged down by a police patrol. He knew at once what had happened: some bored computer operator had slammed his registration number into the system and they'd been alerted by it, though they didn't have a very clear idea why. So they stopped him, asked to see his papers, asked where he was going: they were amiable, unmetropolitan, and entirely happy with his explanation that he was taking a few days' holiday on the coast. They looked cursorily into his bag and found casual clothes, Crabbe's poems, and *No Name* by Wilkie Collins, the book he'd meant to read last time he visited Aldeburgh and would surely fail to again. That had been ages ago. He drove on, vindicated and unnoteworthy, his paranoia beginning to disperse with the cloud.

Perhaps because he seldom had the chance to use them properly, Clive liked roads - not so much the identikit motorways and dual-carriageways, but honest stretches of undulating tarmac with corners, crossroads, strung-out villages and even occasional traffic-jams: roads such as the A12 became when, after the Wickham Market by-pass, it reverted to its once-familiar self. He liked the remnants of railway at Marlesford, the sudden opulence of parkland at Little Glemham, the way in which Farnham closed in with its huddle of buildings, sharp bend and hill before opening out to reveal the anticipated turning and signpost. A1094 Aldeburgh. That had always been the emblematic moment when he felt he was leaving behind not the world exactly but a certain package of debased worldliness. Taking one of of these turnings which led only to a single place and to the North Sea was a particularly deliberate kind of choice, a small exact symbol of the freedom he'd been arguing about with Dylan in the pub on Saturday. According to Jeremy, in one of his more cynical or possibly just more perceptive moods, taking that turning had a couple of distinct practical advantages: you never saw a policeman east of the A12, and the place had its own weather - not necessarily better, but generally more interesting than the stale stuff inland.

And indeed, when the river finally came into view across the meadows to his right, it was glittering in that melancholic, consoling East Anglian sunlight which is like no other light in the world. It had been years, Clive realised, two at least and probably three years since he'd last been here, yet everything felt familiar, in place. Of course, as he reached the outskirts of the town, he began to notice a few changes: there was an unexpected roundabout and a lot of building going on by the Railway Hotel, and an odd little pub, which he surely remembered as The Albert, had at last been converted after years of semi-dereliction into a trendy residence. He drove on downhill and into the town, past the church and over the crossroads to the seafront, parking close to the Moot Hall. He had, just for a moment before meeting Jeremy, to be the simple tourist, to stand and look out at the sea and take a deep breath or two. Punctual as ever, he'd made good time: he wasn't expected for another fifteen minutes. He walked along Crag Path, past the lifeboat, and climbed over the wall onto the shingle. He wanted to stride nonchalantly down to the water's edge, but he'd forgotten how possessively Aldeburgh beach drags you to itself, and his carefree striding soon degenerated into laborious wading, as if through invisible mud. All the same, he thought, all the same. There were gulls and fishing-boats, the onshore breeze was ruffling his hair, and the sunlight was dancing ragged patterns on the water. In his mind he could hear the sparkly one of the Sea Interludes from *Peter Grimes*.

His daydream was interrupted - though so disconcertingly that for a moment he wondered whether the interruption was itself within the daydream - by someone directly behind him singing, in poor imitation of Peter Pears, 'What harbour shelters peace?' He turned round.

'Jeremy!' They fell into a ramshackle slithering hug while Ben gave a couple of doubtful barks. 'I was a bit early, so I thought - '

'You thought you'd make sure the sea was still there.'

'Yes, exactly.'

'I know. I have to do the same when I've only been away for a day. And is it?'

'Is what what?'

'Still there.'

Clive laughed. 'Yes. As ever. Do you doubt it?'

'I sometimes wonder whether it's a mirage. I sometimes wish that fucking thing' - he pointed north along the coast - 'were a mirage.'

'At least that crane's gone. Do you remember? Last time I was here - two, three years ago - there was some kind of huge crane towering over Sizewell. You felt that it might decide to advance down the shore and pick up a whole little town like this one.'

'Well thankfully it didn't. Where's your car by the way?'

'The other side of the Moot Hall. Not on a yellow line.'

'May as well leave it there if it's locked. Is it coffee time or beer time?'

'Between. But I won't feel I've arrived here until I've a pint or two of Adnams' inside me.'

'That's settled then. We'll park the dog at home and go in search of some. And food. Come on, Ben. I thought we might go to Orford for lunch, then I'll cook this evening and we can do the Aldeburgh pubs. Okay?'

'Sounds fine, if you don't mind driving. I'm going to feel too thirsty to risk it, I think.'

'That's settled then.'

They were walking diagonally across the beach towards King Street. Suddenly Clive turned back towards the sea again.

'What amazes me is that it's all so unchanging.'

'I used to think that, but of course it's not true. Everything in the sea and the beach and the sky is moving the whole time. It's because it's continuous that it seems not to change. You notice change far more in an urban environment precisely because there are so many solid things - walls, roofs, roads - which stay much the same. So someone putting up a new sign or painting a door or even breaking a window seems that much more momentous against a background of sameness. Something like that, anyway. I get a bit defensive when people imply that things just stagnate here.'

'Which I didn't.'

'Not quite. How's this famous boy of yours?'

'Kieran? Well, he's not exactly "mine". We had a nice weekend, but now he's buggered off to Copenhagen. He's immensely unreliable, compulsively untruthful even to himself, and altogether too inclined to live dangerously for his good or mine.'

'In other words, you love him.'

'Yes. You know me too well, Jeremy.'

'I know *us* too well. Forty-something and still searching for that key to everything which we somehow mislaid in 1967.'

175

'Do you really believe that?'

For an instant Jeremy looked serious and almost fierce. 'Yes. For ages I thought it was just nostalgia for adolescence - and adolescents. But over the last few years I've heard so many right-wing Tories slagging off the sixties that I reckon we must have had something a bit special then after all. Where we went wrong....' He paused.

'Go on.'

'It sounds so hypocritical, because I want to say that it's not "we" at all, but the rest of them. Where we or they or someone went wrong was in not seeing what would remain after the sixties. I mean, who'd have guessed that a quarter of a century later the world would be saturated with pop music - most of it awful too - but that all the love and idealism would have vanished without trace?'

'I would.'

'Would you really?'

'No, you're right, I suppose I'd have hoped that the ideals might remain while people's taste improved, that we'd end up with a society both good and civilised. That would be asking a bit much, I'm afraid.'

They walked on in silence, across Crag Path and down a tiny side-street to Jeremy's house.

'Was it always that colour?'

'No, it was a sort of ochre. But it's fairly shady here so I thought I'd chance Suffolk pink. It doesn't matter in this street, though if you change the colour of a house on Crag Path people are inclined to mutter a bit. Come in for a second. I only need to dump the dog and get some dosh.'

'You're very rude to him,' said Clive, who didn't much like dogs and was therefore all the more anxious to defend Ben. 'Can't we take him?'

'Not if we're going to Orford. He'll be persecuted by a multitude of Jack Russells in the pub there. He's better off guarding the house than being stuck in the car. Aren't you, Ben?' The dog thumped his tail half-heartedly against the carpet. 'Are we fit?'

'I'll just use your loo,' said Clive, and did so. Some faded stalks of red, pink and white blobs were pressing

176

themselves against the other side of the frosted glass in an alarmingly inquisitive way. He decided they must be hollyhocks.

As he returned, navigating stacks of books in the tiny rear lobby which an estate agent would have called an 'inner hall', he was reminded of the similarly invasive clutter in his office-studio at home.

'You'll have to get a bigger house,' he said, 'or sell some books.'

'All the space I need is out there.' Jeremy grinned ruefully. 'That's the theory anyway.'

'It's a better theory than you know. All through the summer I've been needing that kind of space, without really knowing how or why. I suppose I've always rather suspected the non-urban yearning - at least when I've felt it within myself - as a kind of dishonesty, a sentimental denial of the life I actually have. But now London has become *so* fucking unpleasant, it's like living permanently inside someone else's headache. I don't need that. Anyway, why am I standing here grumbling about London when we should be on our way to a pub?'

'Quite. Be good, Ben. Let's go. Sure you're happy about taking my car?'

'Of course. I promise only to be neurotic about your driving on the way there.'

They walked down King Street to the car park in Oakley Square.

'Still got the Vitesse I see. Must be quite a collectable car by now.'

'It goes. And it stops. And the lid comes off when it's sunny. That's enough for me.'

'All the same, OKE 695 F. I needn't work out the year. 1967?'

'Absolutely. Only trouble is, if you switch on the radio you won't get Johnnie Walker on Radio Caroline and "A Whiter Shade of Pale". Lid on today, I think, don't you?'

'Yes. Too much real air all at once might finish me off.'

On cue, a patch of brilliant sunlight transformed the pastel shades of the colourwashed houses into the vivid tones of a child's paintbox. As they turned into the High Street the still brighter colours of the bunting seemed crazily surreal.

'For me?' said Clive, laughing.

'Carnival weekend. Just in case the tranquility gets too much for you.'

'I don't think it could.'

'Oh yes it bloody well can. Don't sentimentalise it. The quietness, the greyness, the loneliness can be more *continuously* depressing than anything in London. The miseries of urban life can always be countered somehow; you make yourself part of the noise, go to a bar, film, theatre, concert. Here there are times when there's simply no way out of your own head. You can tire of the sound of gulls, too.'

Clive found himself trying to know what Jeremy meant. He did know what Jeremy meant: it was just that, for the moment, although his brain could comprehend what a wet Tuesday afternoon in February might be like in Aldeburgh, his imagination wouldn't stretch to it. They drove on out of the town in silence - he gratefully rediscovered how easy a silence he had always had with Jeremy - and were soon turning off at Snape crossroads towards Orford. As they crossed the bridge and passed the Maltings, a small nostalgic sigh, he couldn't help it, escaped him. It was, after all, a symbol of so much he'd always wanted and never quite achieved: the cultural and the pastoral in exact harmonious balance, itself a monument to a sustained love between two men. His eyes pricked with treacherous tears, and he tried very hard to imagine a dull winter day in Aldeburgh instead.

But as they continued on past Iken and the wide glinting sweep of the river with a distant glimpse of the isolated church on the promontory, it all became too much for him.

'Bloody hell, Jeremy, how dare you live in such a fucking marvellous place?'

'It is, isn't it? Though remember it's partly you being here to see it all afresh which makes it marvellous. I think it's all to do with a way of seeing. What it gives you is

178

potential. There are days, weeks, you can't use it, can't see what it's all about. But at best there's always the space to look, apprehend, regard. Has it ever occurred to you how many metaphors about perception generally are based on seeing?'

'You mean, like "point of view", "see what I mean", "intellectual vision"?'

'Precisely. But remember that all the space can do is give you the potential for seeing. It can't see for you.'

'So the bad times are illuminated with the same unrelieved clarity as the good times?'

'Yes. Frightening, isn't it?'

'Terrifying. But it still sounds okay after London.'

Jeremy smiled. 'Oh yes. After London. Talking of that, there's someone I want you to meet while you're here. He has an interesting perspective on London-and-after, and I'm going to use him as the focus for my *Pendulum* article.'

'Who is he?'

'A writer called William Brannigan who apparently fled to Suffolk in the fifties.'

'Brannigan? I thought he was a famously reclusive lighthouse-keeper or something. Either that or dead.'

'Neither. He's alive and well and good grumbly company. He has grand theories about the death of the city which may even make sense. You'll like him.'

'How very odd. Kieran was talking about writing a book about him the other day.'

'Kieran? Will he ever write a book about anything?'

'I wish I knew. He does worry me. I see him constantly on the edge of self-destruction, and I can't decide whether that's a precondition of genius or just plain ordinary despair. The worst thing is, I keep having to prevent myself from trying to save him.'

'Well, maybe there's hope for you yet.'

'Singular or plural?'

'Both of you. At least you recognise that trying to save someone is the surest way to bugger up a relationship. That's something. And that probably means that you respect him enough to love him.' Jeremy patted Clive's knee. 'About bloody time too.'

'Thanks,' said Clive. 'Man is in love and loves what vanishes.'

'What more is there to say?'

'What indeed?'

*   *   *

It is unquestionably closer to beer time than coffee time when Jeremy stops the car, though doesn't pay for a ticket, in the car park across the road from the Jolly Sailor. From the little market place onwards into Church Street and Quay Street, he has become quietly rapturous, pointing out castle and church, the mellow brick houses and the lush sunken grassy strip along the roadside which was once a creek running up to the crossroads. Things were. And, although he knows that Clive is by now mutinously thirsty, he also knows that the Jolly Sailor isn't to be entered before a quick wander down to the quay itself - past the spruce cottages, and the not-so-spruce, and the one with the infuriating glass bird in the window bobbing its head in a tumbler of water; past the renovated warehouse and the artificial hump in the road which doesn't look to him like a very effective barrier against floodwater although it might be. On the shelter to the right of the quay there's a waist-high marker to show the level of the 1953 flood: it's impressive rather than devastating, because this is, after all, not the sea but the river, taking one last loop inland before the final long straight run to Shingle Street. There are fishing-boats clonking away happily at their moorings, and at the quayside people are coming and going, as they always seem to be, to and from the Lady Florence.

It has charm all right, this scene, but what makes it worthwhile for Jeremy is its refusal to be simply charming. Out on the island-like further shore there are strange pagoda-shaped buildings, military huts, concentration-camp lamp-posts: though the place's use is reputed no longer to be sinister, it will never be pretty. It's real, he says to himself, and then, bafflingly, aloud to Clive: 'All this is

180

real.' Yet Clive smiles, laughing into the breeze, as if he exactly understands - as if, indeed, he is thinking exactly the same thing. Jeremy runs across the little quay towards him, catching and hugging him for a moment. 'Okay,' he says, 'Now for some Adnams' and the most reassuring pub lunch in Suffolk - and that, my dear, is saying something.' They turn back to Quay Street and the pub, although as they do so Jeremy casts a long glance eastwards into the wind, across the river and the shingle spit towards the unceasing North Sea.